DESOLATION CANYON

Jonathan London

Illustrated by

Sean London

WESTWINDS
PRESS®

Library of Congress Cataloging-in-Publication Data
London, Jonathan, 1947-
    Desolation Canyon / by Jonathan London ; illustrated by Sean London.
        pages cm
    Summary: Twelve-year-olds Aaron and Lisa, and sixteen-year-old bad-boy
Cassidy, join their Army-buddy fathers on a float trip down Utah's Green
River, where they face terrible physical and mental challenges.
    ISBN 978-1-941821-29-9 (pbk.)
    ISBN 978-1-941821-55-8 (e-book)
    ISBN 978-1-941821-60-2 (hardbound)
    [1. Adventure and adventurers—Fiction. 2. White-water canoeing—
Fiction. 3. Rafting (Sports)—Fiction. 4. Interpersonal relations—Fiction. 5.
Green River (Wyo.-Utah)—Fiction.] I. London, Sean, illustrator. II. Title.
    PZ7.L8432Des 2015
    [Fic]—dc23
                              2014025857

Editor: Michelle McCann
Designer: Vicki Knapton

Published by WestWinds Press®
An imprint of

GRAPHIC ARTS
BOOKS®

P.O. Box 56118
Portland, Oregon 97238-6118
503-254-5591
www.graphicartsbooks.com

For Roger, Lisa, Rowan, Dennis, Skip, Max, Steve, &
Natalia—and the whole Mountain White Water gang—
all friends of the Green River. And as always to my wife,
sweet Maureen. With thanks to Avi. And with special
thanks to my son Aaron, whose journal of our week on
the Green River was invaluable; and to my son Sean,
whose journal of another white-water rafting adventure
we shared was also a revelation.

—Jonathan London

To Dad and Aaron, for blazing the trail, to my mom
and my wife, Stephanie, for their love and support, and
to Roger and Lisa, for all the adventures.

—Sean London

CONTENTS

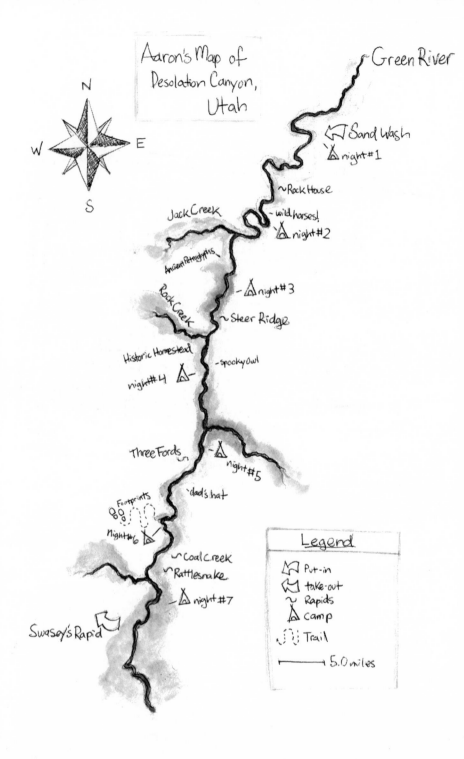

CHAPTER ONE

WHITE WATER!

Cassidy lifted a huge stone on the clifftop high over my head. He glared down at me, laughed with crazy glee, and dropped it. I leaped away. The water burst white behind me, and I crashed into the river. A swirling dark hole funneled down, down, dragging me with it.

Coyotes on the canyon rim woke me up—or was it Cassidy's dad, Wild Man Willie, yowling, "Come 'n' get it!"?

Dad groaned, and I gazed at the ghosts of the nightmare still floating around inside our tent.

"Come on, Aaron," Dad muttered, and we crawled out of our tent and followed our noses.

At the camp kitchen, I picked up an enamel plate from a stack, shoveled piles of food on it, and sat down on a stump. Still dazed by the dream, I dug into the pancakes and bacon and watched Wild Man Willie make a pot of coffee—army style. Big old coffeepot filled with boiling water and tons of coffee grounds. He took it by the handle and spun it round and round, like a windmill.

"Separates the grounds from the coffee," Willie growled. If that pot flew off the handle, someone could get killed.

Dad told me that Willie had been a squad leader during Desert Storm, the first Iraq war, way back in 1991. Dad had met him and Roger the Rogue in the army, when they were all young. Now the three buddies were ex-soldiers, on one of their annual white-water rafting trips down wild rivers. This year it was the Green River in Desolation Canyon, deep in the Utah desert. Dad had told me it was one of the most remote places in the lower forty-eight states.

This was my first time white-water rafting. Willie's son Cassidy, who was four years older than me, had gone on lots of rafting trips. And the only other kid, Roger's daughter Lisa, had too. I was the only newbie on the trip. It was the first week of April, and like me, Lisa was missing a week of sixth grade to go rafting (and there were only seven weeks left when we got home!).

"Where's Cassidy?" asked Roger. His eyes twinkled above a wicked goatee. He shoved his long curly hair beneath his spotted red bandanna.

"C-A-A-A-S-S-I-I-I-D-Y-Y-Y!" howled Wild Man Willie.

Only the river called back, a quiet hiss.

Willie dashed the last of his coffee into the sand and leaped barefoot through prickles and stones toward Cassidy's tent. With his huge arms he heaved the back of the tent up and over and dumped Cassidy out the open door, still curled up in his boxers.

Lisa laughed and covered her mouth.

It felt a little weird seeing Cassidy there after just having a nightmare about him.

Cassidy just lay there. One eye opened. Then the other.

Then he rolled back into a handspring and landed like a cat in the warm sand.

Lisa clapped. Something twisted in my heart. Here's this girl—maybe the cutest girl I've ever seen, long and slender, with what looked like a permanent tan—flinging her black ponytail back and applauding Cassidy, a bad kid if there ever was one.

Dad had told me all about him, warned me to watch out for him. Said he'd been in a juvenile detention center for bashing a man's head with a baseball bat when he was only fourteen, two years older than I am now. Dad told me his mother had died when he was little and that Willie "had his hands full with this one."

Cassidy stood up and wiped sand from his body. He was burnt lobster red after spending all day yesterday in the hot sun. His muscles coiled like snakes as he brushed his body clean. His tattoos rippled. He was crawling with tattoos!

"Let's get this show on the road!" Willie said. "You missed breakfast."

"I ain't hungry," Cassidy said.

"Now!" growled Willie.

Cassidy picked up his sleeping bag and wrapped it around his head and body so only his eyes peered out. Lisa grinned.

"Pronto!" Willie barked.

Like yesterday—our first day on the river, after a night at the put-in at Sand Wash—it took about an hour to break camp, pump air into the three big inflatable rafts, strap down any gear that could bounce off in the rapids, and take off.

Yesterday it was a slow, lazy river, with lots of hard rowing. Dad was teaching me how. These rafts had long oars instead of paddles, and you had to put your legs and back into each long pull. Like yesterday, here the river was flat. As I rowed there was plenty of time to gaze up at the high reddish-brown walls of the canyon, topped with magnificent buttes and towers.

And there was plenty of time to get bored.

As if reading my mind, Dad said, "You're gonna love it

today, kiddo. And by the end of the trip, you're gonna learn to read the river like a pro."

Read the river? I wasn't sure what that meant, but I figured I'd soon find out.

The river started to get faster. It seemed to suck us along. I was facing backwards at the oars, so I was forced to twist my neck around to see where I was going and what was coming.

Then I heard it.

"Listen," Dad said.

"What is it?" I asked.

"White water!" he shouted.

That's when I felt the fear. Like a horse kicked me in the chest. I could feel a cold spray.

Then, all of a sudden, the water was white, as if thousands of snowy rabbits were jumping all around us. My heart danced in my stomach.

"You can do this, Aaron!" Dad said, "I really think you can do this!"

But I didn't think I could do this. I wanted to push the oars away. I wanted to jump out of my skin.

I tried to row, but the water just shoved us wherever it wanted us to go. I could hardly keep the boat straight, let alone steer. I wrestled with the oars for a bit, then yelled, *"YAAAAAAAAAH!"*

Finally, Dad tapped my shoulder. He was going to take over.

As I stood up to let him take over, I lost my grip on the right oar and it ripped out of my hand. The handle conked me in the head.

And my mind went black.

CHAPTER TWO

THE WILD BUNCH

I was drowning.

I was flailing and fighting and kicking and gagging. I tried to scream, but water filled my mouth. I couldn't see a thing and my body was spinning round and round and bouncing, churning inside one of nature's giant washing machines.

Maytag! Maytag! rang through my head. *Which way was up?*

I was terrified as I tumbled down the river, eyes closed, fighting for air, juggling snapshots of my short life.

Suddenly, I was snatched up, as if by a giant eagle.

Dad had grabbed me by my lifejacket and heaved me up. Next thing I knew, I was sprawled on the bottom of the raft, belching water.

"What happened?" I spluttered.

"You fell in. Are you okay?" Dad took off his straw hat, and the sun behind him made a halo around his bearded bony face, his nest of hair.

My head was throbbing. I reached up and brushed the wet mop of hair aside and felt the golf ball poking up beneath the skin of my forehead.

"You took a spill," Dad said, and pulled me up beside him. "Nasty bump you got there, kiddo." He smiled and adjusted the hawk feather in his hatband, and put his hat back on.

We were floating lazily down another long, smooth stretch of river now. I looked around. There was Wild Man Willie, not twenty feet away, in the "kitchen boat," where we kept all the food and cooking supplies. He was laughing like a loon. It was so embarrassing. I'd fallen in on my first rapid.

"Took a nosedive on your first Class 3, huh, pard?" he said. "Thought your dad had caught him a big trout, the way you were flopping around in the bottom of that boat!"

I didn't say anything. What could I say?

Beside him Cassidy just hunkered, grinning and

shaking his head. "Hey, fool," he said. "Better buckle your seat belt next time!" Har har.

I looked away. Bully. He acted like the bullies at school. They liked to embarrass people, too.

I was embarrassed plenty.

Lisa was up ahead in the lead raft with her father, standing and staring at me. I couldn't tell in the sun-glare if she was smiling or worried or what. I'm sure my face turned redder than the sun had already burned it.

I rubbed my head again. And I rubbed my right shoulder, which felt like it had been yanked out of its socket.

"On a scale of five," Dad said, "Class 3 is just a taste of what's to come downriver. There's real fun to be had. But next time, if you can't handle it—though I think you can—hang on to that oar till I can take over. Okay, kiddo?"

Now you tell me, Dad, I wanted to say sarcastically. But I just sat there frozen, sunk into myself. If this was "just a taste of what's to come," I was in for it.

I was still catching my breath—visualizing Cassidy ridiculing me—when I heard Roger holler, "Pull out!"

Sitting around on a sandy beach, chowing down lunch, Cassidy spun his baseball cap backwards on his head and said, "Willie"—that's what he called his dad—"What was that you were saying the other day about the Wild Bunch?"

Willie crouched down in the sand before the three of us—Cassidy, Lisa, and me. In his floppy, battered hat, he looked like a short, powerful, crocodile wrestler with a big belly hard as iron.

"I was saying how Butch Cassidy and his Wild Bunch used to use this here canyon—Desolation Canyon—for their escape routes after robbing banks back in the late eighteen hundreds."

"You mean like Butch Cassidy and the Sundance Kid, right?"

Butch Cassidy and the Sundance Kid. I'd seen the DVD last summer with my dad. A good old movie with a bad ending, if I remembered right. Bad for the "heroes," anyway. I think they both died in a shoot-out.

"Not exactly like in the movies," said Willie. "But legends about the Wild Bunch grew faster than desert flowers after a cloudburst. Law was always after them, and half the time folks were on the outlaws' side. You wouldn't want to get on their wrong side."

I snatched a look at Willie's son, with his thick muscles and sinister tattoos. *Same name. Was he named after Butch Cassidy? And does that make us part of the Wild Bunch in his twisted imagination?*

I didn't feel like sitting around anymore. I hopped up and wandered over to the water's edge. The Green River swirled lazily by.

Suddenly, I was up in the air, then soaring out into the river. It was so cold and I was so surprised that I practically danced on the water. I didn't even have time to yell.

I stood up in the shallows and splashed back to shore, gasping, laughing or crying, I'm not sure which. Cassidy greeted me with a nasty grin, more like a sneer. He was missing a couple of teeth, which made him look even more menacing.

He reached out and yanked me up on the bank. "Geez! Watch it!" I yelled. A knife of pain seared my sore shoulder. He was only sixteen years old, but he had arms like a WWE wrestler on TV, with tattoos of knives and snakes coiled around his arms and chest.

"Guess you slipped, dude," he said.

"Yeah, whatever," I said, rubbing my right shoulder. I didn't know what to say. Everybody was looking at me.

Lisa was looking at me.

At school, I tried to ignore the bullies. Here, I couldn't ignore Cassidy. I tried to hide my frustration and embarrassment.

My dad walked over to Cassidy. "That was a little rough, don't ya think?" He picked up a small flat stone and skipped it across the water.

"Dude! What's your problem?" snapped Cassidy.

Dad was trying to stand up for me, but he was just embarrassing me even more. He stared hard at Cassidy for a moment, then strolled off, down along the river.

Cassidy picked up a perfect skipping stone and fired it so hard it blurred across the water, bouncing six . . . seven . . . eight times.

Wow, I said to myself. I picked up a skipping stone and flashed it sidearm across the water. A slash of pain shot up my shoulder. The rock bounced once, then plunked and sank out of sight. *Great*, I thought. *Just great.*

Cassidy just grinned.

The river was silent. I rubbed my shoulder and felt pretty dumb. *Why couldn't I be like Cassidy? But without all the macho and menace?*

Suddenly Willie (I guess to break the awkward silence) picked Cassidy up, swung him around, and tossed him out into the river. He screeched and landed with a splash.

Then went under.

But he didn't pop back up like I had. After a few long moments, even I started to get a bad feeling. *Did he get pulled downriver? Had he hit his head and gotten KOed by a boulder? Was he drowning?*

Before I could come up with more worst-case scenarios, Cassidy erupted from the water about one hundred feet downriver. Laughing. He was laughing like a monkey, splashing and jumping up and down. He jumped up and caught a low limb overhanging the water, swung like a chimpanzee, and flew off, back into the river.

Then he swam back to us and stomped up to shore.

And came tearing straight at me.

I tried to juke him, like in a football game.

But at the last second he swerved and lifted his dad up

in the air like a bodybuilder, and swung him high and hard out into the river. Willie made even a bigger splash than Cassidy had.

He bounced back up from the bottom, and stared at Cassidy, murder in his eyes. Then he laughed, deep and hearty, and slashed the water with a powerful hand, spraying all of us standing on the shore. He yelled to Cassidy, "I'm comin' to get ya!"

"Really, old man?" said Cassidy. "Good luck with that!"

Willie started wading in toward Cassidy, and at the same time, Roger yelled, "Yahoo!" and lurched toward Lisa to throw her in.

She leaped away just in time, ran over and slapped my shoulder. "Race ya!" she yelled and took off down the beach. I took off after her.

My river shoes squelched. I'm fast but she was faster. She tore down the beach like a cheetah and soon flew, on her long legs, around the bend and out of sight. This didn't exactly help my self-esteem, but it was fun, and better than getting tossed in the river by Cassidy.

I followed her to the end of the beach. Great chunks of stone littered the foot of the canyon walls. Up above, you could see dark caves in the red canyon rock. Lisa started up, angling up across the cliff face, finding handholds and footholds on every tiny ledge. I followed.

"Watch out for mountain lions!" I hollered. Roger had warned us that there were cougars in this country. Lisa climbed like a wildcat, sending sharp little flecks of stone into my face and hair.

By the time we reached the first cave, sweat stung my eyes. It's always scary stepping into a dark place, but Lisa led the way. It was cool inside the darkness of the cave, and at first I was glad because it was scorching hot out. But soon an icy shiver ran up and down my spine, as much from the spookiness as the wet T-shirt clinging to me. We stood in the darkness for a while, rubbing the chill from our arms.

"We shoulda brought a flashlight," I said.

"I like the dark," Lisa said. "It's kinda, like, cozy in here, don't you think?"

Wow, I thought. *Is she flirting with me? Should I make a move? And what move would that be?*

That's when I heard something echo through the cave. *Was it a footstep? Was something following us?* My hair prickled, my muscles tensed.

ROAAAAAAARRRRRRRRRR!

Lisa and I jumped about three feet straight up and then fell all over each other trying to get out of the cave.

But a dark shadow blocked the entrance.

CHAPTER THREE

ROCK SLIDE AND HIGH SIDE

The shadow crouched.

Then laughed like a hyena.

Of course, it was Cassidy. He hadn't waited around to be thrown into the river again. He'd followed us up. I tried to laugh too, to act like he hadn't scared me. But it came out more like a croak. I didn't realize that Lisa had been hugging me hard from behind until she let go.

"That was mean!" she yelled. Then she sprinted toward him like she was going to knock him down.

He caught her in a bear hug. "Let go, you creep!" she said. She giggled and squirmed. I couldn't believe it, but she was acting like she kind of liked it, like she was flirting. I felt that knife twisting in my heart again. I pushed by them, out into the hot blast of sun.

I started climbing down to the river. "Wait up!" Lisa called as she scrambled down behind me. Cassidy stayed up at the cave, watching us.

As we neared the bottom, small pebbles and stones started rolling and ricocheting past us. I looked back up. Cassidy was lobbing rocks down at us! Just as we reached the bottom, this little avalanche started chasing us.

"Hey!" I yelled, "you trying to kill somebody?"

Lisa came tearing by me on those long brown legs of hers. She was crying.

No, she was laughing. How could she laugh?

I scratched my head, then took off after her.

After a while, I wasn't exactly laughing—I was too winded to laugh—but I was actually starting to enjoy myself again. Lisa ran, I followed. I tried to catch up. I couldn't, but almost.

Soon I had forgotten about Cassidy and was just running on my aching legs in the hot vastness of this great canyon. It felt good.

Back at the beach, Roger, Dad, and Wild Man Willie were loading up the rafts. I heard a hum like a bee's buzz and looked up, shielding my eyes from the sun. Far overhead, above the flattop of a nearby mesa, I saw a small single-engine plane. It tilted and circled once, then zoomed down and seemed to disappear into rock.

"Let's get this show on the road!" bellowed Willie. "Where's Cassidy?"

About twenty minutes later Cassidy came sauntering down. "Did you see it, dude?" he asked me.

"See what?"

"The mountain lion. *GRRRRRRRROWWWLLL!*" He made a little swipe with his hand, like a clawed paw.

Lisa giggled. I tried to smile. It was almost funny.

Back on the river, it was so slow that Roger decided to lash our rafts together and just float for a while.

Willie lobbed oranges at us from the ice chest on his boat. Then he flew big flat cookies at us like Frisbees, and chucked some cans of soda.

I leaped over to Roger and Lisa's raft and flopped down beside her on some big squishy "dry bags" filled with clothes.

"Mind if I join you?" I asked.

"If you don't hog all the goodies," she said. Then she shoved me and I almost toppled back into the river.

I grinned and took a deep breath. *This is fun!* I thought. Here we are, deep in a canyon drifting down a river through the wild desert, with rock pillars standing like guard towers on a ruined castle . . . and there's a girl flirting with me. And she seems to maybe like me, a little. Me. Aaron. I'm kind of scrawny—but not weak, I'm not weak—lanky, with brown eyes that I'd like to think are deep, even mysterious maybe. I'm just a little shy around girls, and yet this really hot girl seems to like me. And maybe even thinks I'm, well, kinda cute. I think.

I hope. Or is she just playing with me?

Suddenly, Cassidy leaped over from the kitchen boat and practically landed in Lisa's lap.

"Get off me, you moron!" She shoved him off, but she was laughing as she did it.

Cassidy popped open a can of Sprite. It sprayed all over me.

"Really? Spaz," I said.

He looked at me like he was going to bite my head off, then took a long slurp, and said, "Last time I went white-water rafting, a boat ahead of us wrapped around a pillar in some super crazy rapids under a bridge."

I was still angry at him for raining an avalanche down on us, but I couldn't help but ask, "Geez. So . . . what happened?"

"Everybody was thrown out, man," he said, taking another swig. "Except one. The guide."

"What happened to him?"

"He bit it, dude." Cassidy grinned and pierced me with those eyes of his.

"Seriously?" Lisa and I both said it at the same time. We

looked at each other. I thought she was going to punch me. I looked back at Cassidy. Maybe he was just pulling our leg, but if he was, it was a pretty good act.

"Yeah, his leg got caught under the safety line that runs down the middle of the raft. And he's all like, 'HELP! I'm stuck!' When the raft wrapped around the pylon, it pulled the line tight and trapped his leg. When the raft went under it held him underwater. He drowned. I saw it. Willie jumped in with a knife to cut the line, but he was too late."

"Oh my God! That's a terrible story!" cried Lisa, grabbing my arm.

"I think it was wicked, dude," Cassidy just burped. "Danger gives you power," he said. "Or takes it away. It makes you feel alive, dude." He crumpled his soda can and tossed it in the river. He stared at us, his steely eyes like ball bearings.

Lisa and I glanced at each other. Her eyes seemed to be saying, *How are we going to survive this trip with a nutcase like him along?* I couldn't help but to think how much more fun this trip would be without him.

"Hop to, mates!" Roger yelled. "We're coming up on some fast water!"

Cassidy and I each jumped back to our rafts and helped break them free, and we were on our way.

Soon, Roger called for a pull-out to scout the rapids. I used this opportunity to relieve myself behind a rock pile. I'd glugged a ton of water after our climb to the cave.

When they got back, Dad reminded me about "high-siding." Meaning, you have to climb to the high side of a raft if it gets pressed up against a boulder and starts riding up it. "And tighten your lifejacket, kiddo. If you fall in, try to go through the rapids feetfirst, so you can bounce off the boulders."

Bounce off the boulders? I gulped. I didn't know if I could face another plunge into the rapids. And I didn't know which was worse, the possibility of drowning or the torment of Cassidy's ridicule.

Dad rowed. I sat high on the tube at the back. Ours was the last boat in line. I heard the roar and could see a line of white up ahead. Mist rose above the boulders. Just the sound made my whole body tense up.

"Hold on tight, kiddo!" Dad said. He swung the raft around to see what we were facing, which put me in front, on the bow. I was looking right down at the rapids, like at the start of a roller-coaster drop. *Yiiiiikes!*

I took another deep breath. Cassidy's story haunted me, but really, I was almost starting to love this—the thrill of it, like you could love and dread a roller-coaster ride at the same time.

But then I deflated again, small with fear, when I saw Roger the Rogue's raft being swept into the rapids ahead of us, and Lisa's ponytail flying like a black banner as they dropped out of sight.

Then Willie and Cassidy disappeared into the roaring spray.

Our turn now. *Oh, God! Oh, God! Here it comes!*

I was more afraid the closer we got. Yet I felt as wide-awake as you can be, ready for anything. At least, I thought I was. I gripped the safety rope that rings the top of the boat with all my might.

"We have to stay left of that big boulder there, Aaron," Dad shouted. "If we hit it and the raft rides up it, jump to the high side of the raft. With luck, we'll slide back down. If not, we'll wrap!" The image of the guide who drowned flashed through my mind.

The image of *me* almost drowning flashed too.

All of a sudden the river went wild. Waves reared up like white stallions and crashed in a thunder of hooves. Water churned and twisted and burst off rocks. I clenched my teeth and fists as we whipped and spun and bounced.

"*Yee-HA!*" I whooped. It felt like I was riding a bucking bronco. "Hey, this is fu—*Whoops!*" I almost toppled backwards into the boat, but grabbed the safety rope and held on.

We were racing toward the boulder. It was huge and shiny black, the water pouring over it in a smooth, fast gleam of power, then crashing into a big foaming hole on the far side.

"Hang on tight!" Dad shouted again, and I did.

Oh God, I'm gonna die!

Just as we came near the boulder, Dad dug his right oar into the river and spun us around. We were sliding toward the rock. Water was exploding around it. We were bucking and lurching and all of a sudden the boulder was in my face. It reminded me of the time Dad spun out of control on an icy road in the Sierras on a ski trip and we slid toward a snowbank.

Like then, I instinctively leaned away, tensed for disaster. Our raft started riding up the boulder and I jumped to the low side of the raft, away from the boulder. In my panic I was making things worse.

We were going to wrap!

"High side, Aaron!" Dad hollered. *"High side!"*

CHAPTER FOUR

WILD HORSES

High side, Aaron!" Dad shouted again.

Dad's words finally sank in. I crawled up on the high side of the raft and braced my feet against the opposite tube, my hands holding on to the safety rope for dear life.

The river pressed us against the rock like a postage stamp. But I was pressing down from the high side, and finally my weight—along with Dad's—forced the raft to slide down . . . slowly . . . slowly . . .

. . . until the current caught enough of the raft to whip us around the boulder, and away, downstream.

"Yahoo!" I yelled. Geez, that felt good.

"Good job, kiddo!" Dad yelled. My heart pumped into all my veins until I swelled with pride.

Our raft wobbled and rolled and slid off waves until the rapids died and the river flattened out once again.

"That was awesome, Dad!" It was awesome and it was scary. My heart still thundered in my chest.

"You did great, kiddo," he said. "And there's more like it to come!"

"Sweet," I said, a little dubiously. I looked ahead to see if Lisa was watching. She was leaning over the side of their raft, slapping water at Cassidy. Cassidy shook a can of soda and sprayed her, laughing like a maniac.

But I wasn't going to let them bother me. I was proud, and I didn't care about anyone else.

At least, that's what I tried to tell myself.

It was getting late and we were starting to look for a place to camp along the bank when Roger yelled, "Horses! Wild horses!"

There on the steep slope that rose toward the canyon walls to our left were five horses and one young colt grazing in the snake grass. You could see their muscles twitching and bulging. The lead stallion swung his huge head, stomped his front hoof, and took off running. The others followed, hooves pounding, rocks sliding. The little colt—a pinto—chased behind, struggling to keep up.

Wild horses. Mustangs! They were fast and shaggy and fierce. They angled up the bank and off in a cloud of dust.

And for a long time I could still feel the pounding of those hoofs. It was like the pounding of my heart as we'd gone down those rapids.

We finally found a good place, on a sandy bank among cottonwoods, to set up camp. My cut-offs were soaked so I was glad to change into sweatpants once we got settled.

I had some free time and sat alone on the bank beneath a big old cottonwood. I listened to the river chuckle and chatter, and studied the beauty of the high canyon walls in the reddish-gold sun. It was a good time to jot in the journal Mrs. P asked me to keep about my trip, for missing a week of school. I wrote: "April 3," and after describing the canyon ("massive amphitheaters of sandstone . . .") I started to describe the day. And what a day it had been—white water and wild horses!

And then for the first time on this trip, I thought about my mom. And even Sean, my little brother! How I wished they could have seen me rafting down those rapids with flying colors.

Mom's a nurse at a hospital north of San Francisco and couldn't get off work. Sean is eight, and Dad thought he was still too young for a trip like this. Especially without Mom being here to help.

Honestly, Mom probably could've gotten the time off, if she really wanted to. We all knew she loved to float rivers and enjoy the beauty of nature, but she didn't like big rapids at all. They scared her. And she really didn't like camping out on sandy beaches all that much. "Sand in my sandwich!" she would say. Sand in her sleeping bag. Sand in her hair. Sand everywhere.

But Sean, he would've loved this. He's not afraid of anything. He would've wanted to be up front in the bow of the raft the entire time, with waves slamming into him, yelling, *"Hi-YAH!"* like he was going to battle each one as it came.

And those wild horses! He would've drawn them for sure! He's a wizard with a pen and paper. Or pencil or crayons or a paintbrush. He's always drawing. He takes a drawing pad with him everywhere he goes.

I hadn't really been afraid about coming on this rafting trip until today when I'd had my first bout with the rapids and lost. Geez, I could've drowned. I could've bit it. Rapids are like bullies, sometimes. They like to pound you and make you feel small. Grind you up and spit you out.

But rapids could be a blast, too. I was starting to see that now. I didn't want to see those other images anymore, which had flooded my mind. Those images of drowning.

Wild Man Willie's call to *"Come 'n' get it!"* rang off the cliffs, and man, was I starved! He had made Mexican food. We had tortilla chips to dip into guacamole and salsa, shrimps too, then tortillas to roll up heaps of beans, rice, chicken, and grated cheese. Yum!

As my grandpa used to say, "Life is good. Life is good."

That night around the fire, I watched the flames dance, and listened again to the sound of the river. I thought about the wild horses, and felt again the rush of something surging through me—with the power of the horses, the power of the river.

I peered over at Lisa, on the far side of the fire. I wanted to talk to her—to share my thoughts—but just when I finally got up the nerve, Cassidy asked her if she wanted to play cards in his tent. She glanced at me, and for a moment my heart stopped. What was a twelve-year-old girl doing hanging out with a sixteen-year-old boy? It made me mad, but I didn't say anything. She shrugged and got up and followed him to his tent. I could have joined them, I guess, but I couldn't move. I was frozen in place. I gazed into the fire as it collapsed in on itself.

What would I have said to her anyway? What could we talk about? I'm pretty smart, and at school I'm good at writing, but who wants to talk about that? I play soccer and flag football and Little League baseball, and I do pretty well—especially at baseball. But I'm pretty sure she doesn't want to talk about sports either. Or bullies, which I try to dodge like flying tacklers.

I want to get to know her and for her to know me, but those things don't define me. Who I am.

Who am I?

I'm simple. Or maybe not so simple. I'm not a nerd or a jock. I really just want to be liked. By girls, I mean. But I never know what to say to them. Maybe I should write Lisa my thoughts, instead of trying to talk to her. But really, it would be too embarrassing. "Here, Lisa, read this. I wrote you my thoughts."

She probably would laugh in my face, and say, "You dork!"

I really don't know what I want to be when I grow up. Not yet. For a while I wanted to be a pro baseball player. That idea didn't last too long. Now I'm thinking maybe a paleontologist digging up dinosaur bones. Or maybe a celebrity chef with my own show on the Food Network. That would be cool.

Only, I don't really know how to cook. And I'm not that into dinosaurs anymore.

I think really, to be liked by somebody, you first have to like yourself. Does that make sense?

I'm not sure.

Those were some of the thoughts that swirled around my brain as I dragged myself to our tent.

After a while Dad climbed in beside me. I'd lit our lantern and was trying to finish my journal entry, but every time I heard Lisa and Cassidy laughing in his tent, I lost my train of thought. Dad wanted to talk, so I let him. I wasn't listening, not to him. I put my journal and pen away and said, "I'm tired, Dad. I'm going to sleep now."

"Goodnight, kiddo. Fun day, huh? The rapids. And then those wild horses! I wish your mom was here. And Sean. They would've loved that!"

"'Night, Dad." It was a fun day, but I felt too mixed up to say anything.

I rolled away and closed my eyes.

I was dreaming about wild horses—I couldn't see them, just hear them, the thunder of their hooves—when my eyes popped back open.

Lisa was squealing with laughter.

CHAPTER FIVE

NIGHTMARE ROCK

By nine the next morning we were on the river again. This time I rode with Roger the Rogue and Lisa, while Dad joined Cassidy, and Willie went solo. I wanted to say to Lisa, "Did you two have fun playing cards last night?" but I knew it would come out sounding weird.

It was an easy stretch of river, so Roger let Lisa row for a while, then me. Within a few minutes, we had pulled far ahead of Dad, who was doing the rowing while Cassidy lounged in back.

"Heave ho, matey!" barked Roger like a pirate captain. "Put your back into it, Aaron!" There was a slight headwind building, so I did have to pull harder to keep us moving.

Roger named the plants as we slid by: cottonwoods and cattails growing along the river's edge, and up the dry, sparsely covered slopes. All kinds of desert shrubs like sage-brush, skunkbush, greasewood, and spiny yucca. Here and there sparse forests of pinyon pine and juniper were cling-ing tenaciously to the high slopes and cliffs.

I spotted a couple of flying squirrels soaring between trees, and atop a low ridge we saw a group of bighorn sheep. High overhead floated a golden eagle, rising slowly up a thermal into the sun.

I'd been rowing long and hard when Cassidy pulled up alongside our boat (he'd taken over rowing from my dad). With an evil grin on his face, he dropped the oars and started pumping me with a huge water gun. The water was freezing cold and I ducked down, laughing like a loon, searching madly for something to use to get back at him.

Roger hollered, "Water fight! Water fight!" and madness broke loose! Roger heaved a bail bucket full of river water back at Cassidy, dousing him from head to toe. Then, from behind me—*whoosh!* I was soaked and saw Lisa standing over me with an empty, dripping bucket. I grabbed her around the knees and she toppled into the river. She splashed and swore and shook her fist at me.

"I'm gonna get you, Aaron! I'm gonna kick your butt!"

"Oh yeah? You and whose army?" I yelled, grinning from ear to ear.

SPLAT! Cassidy nailed me with another water gun blast. But then Wild Man Willie jumped into Dad's raft, grabbed the water gun from Cassidy, and started pumping me and Roger. Laughing like a maniac, he tossed the water gun over to Roger and taunted him, "Hey Rambo! Bet you couldn't hit the broad side of a barn with a handful of—"

SPLAT! Roger nailed him right in the chest. Willie faked

a gunshot to the heart and toppled forward into the river, almost on top of Lisa, just as Dad jumped over to row Willie's kitchen boat before it went downriver on its own.

Not wanting to be left out of the fun, I jumped into the river, dove under, grabbed Lisa by the legs, and gave them a yank.

Big mistake! She glubbed and blubbed back up to the surface—then slapped her hand on top of my head like an eagle's talons, and dunked me, holding me under until I twisted free. By the time I thrashed back to the surface, she was climbing into the raft, out of my reach. Next thing I knew, she was pumping me with the water gun. *SPLAT! SPLAT! SPLAT!*

I'm a pretty good swimmer, so I dove under her raft. She couldn't see me through the silty, snowmelt water, so when I silently popped up on the other side of the raft, right below where she was sitting, she had no idea where I was. She was looking for me in the water on the other side. Her leg was dangling overboard, so I grabbed it and pulled her, shrieking, back into the water.

She was just trying to dunk me again when Roger called a truce. It was time to pull in. Just to play it safe, I climbed back into the kitchen raft with my dad.

Roger, Dad, and Cassidy eddied out their respective rafts and tied them off to a bunch of river willows on shore. It was time to eat lunch.

Willie and Roger pulled out the folding legs on the

kitchen table and started setting up. After checking to make sure Lisa wasn't following me, I ducked behind a boulder, stripped off my wet clothes, and put on my swimming trunks.

As I walked back toward the table, I could hear Dad talking to Willie. "I hate to have to say this, Willie," Dad was telling him, "but you need to talk to your son about his mouth. Before the water fight, Cassidy and I had a little spat and it wasn't pretty. I won't repeat the foul words he used, but basically he didn't like the way I was rowing, said I rowed like an old lady. I told him, 'Here, you row,' and he grabbed the oars and started rowing like there was a war raging inside him."

Willie crinkled his face as if there was a bright light hurting his eyes. "Ever since his mother died he's had a hair-trigger temper." Willie stopped talking when he saw Lisa come running at me. She was in her bathing suit now too, and she was coming fast.

Uh-oh! I sprinted as hard as I could down the beach. Around a bend, I found myself plopping through deep mud where a spring ran down to the river. Lisa was gaining fast. I could hear her slopping through the muck right behind me.

"Mud fight!" she yelled, as she did a flying tackle at my legs, toppling me over. *SPLAT!* I hit the mud, and before I could get up, she was on my back pushing my face into the brown goo.

Oh no! I thought, in a panic. *I'm getting beat up by a girl!*

I managed to roll over so she slid off me, but she sprang back up and pounced on my chest. This girl was fast!

"Eat this!" she said, grabbing a handful of mud. She was laughing and it was like her dark eyes laughed, too. And her hair hung down all scraggly in her face, with little blobs of mud sticking in it.

"Get off!" I hollered. I tried grabbing her wrists but my hands were too slippery. She was leaning over pushing the handful of mud toward my face when we heard something behind us. My dad said, "Freeze!" and Lisa stopped wrestling and whipped around toward his voice.

I took the opportunity to push her knees up and knock her over backwards into the mud. I jumped up and pulled her arm like I was going to help her up, then let her fall face first into the mud.

Dad laughed and took a picture of us half-wrestling and half-hugging, giggling and slap-happy, like two mud sculptures come to life.

"Thanks, kids!" Dad said, then ran back down the beach.

Then, all of a sudden I was on my back again. Lisa had me pinned and was chanting, "Eat this! Eat this!" while holding a big glob of mud over my face.

Again, someone said, "Freeze!"—but this time the voice came from above us.

And it wasn't my dad.

It was Cassidy. He was standing on the cliff above us, looking down at us. Leering. And he was lifting a huge rock over his head.

It was just like the nightmare rock—that rock in the nightmare I'd had our first night on the river.

And I knew in my bones he was about to drop that rock right on us.

CHAPTER SIX

ROCK ART AND RATTLERS

Cassidy stood against the sky, and with a crazy yell—
"Aaiiiiiiii-yaaaah!"—he heaved the rock (it was twice
the size of a boom box!) right down at the two of us. I closed
my eyes and we both screamed. We didn't have time
to move.

Then—*ker-SPLASH!*—the rock crashed into the river a
few feet behind us. My eyes were still closed, but it was so
close that the splash soaked us both with icy water.

I opened my eyes to see Lisa kneeling beside me, breathing hard. She looked like a mud statue of a girl praying. My
heart was galloping like that band of wild horses.

Lisa was glaring up at Cassidy and he was glaring right
back down at us. Was he trying to hit us? I wondered. Or
did he just want to scare us? If that was his goal, he'd
succeeded.

A third yell broke the spell.

It was my dad again. He was swearing at Cassidy, yelling at the top of his lungs. And my dad wasn't much of a

swearer. Cassidy gave him a thumbs-up sign, then disappeared behind the rocks above.

Lisa sighed, stood up, and slowly walked back toward camp, her eyes downcast.

I could see Willie talking to my dad. My dad was shaking his head. I jumped into the river to wash the mud off and to try and cleanse my mind of that menace that had seeped into my little mud pool of happiness.

Shivering with goose bumps, I climbed out and joined Dad and the others at the kitchen table. My stomach felt queasy but I was still starving. I slapped together a big fat sandwich and chomped down. Lisa sat alone at the river's edge, her feet dangling in the water. Willie came over and plopped a big arm over my shoulders.

"Hey, pard. How ya doin'?"

I just shrugged and chewed my sandwich.

"Cassidy's just a prankster—a big practical joker," he said. "Last time we were in a mountain canyon like this he helped me pry a pole beneath a half-ton boulder and roll it off a cliff. It made a splash like a bomb exploding!"

"Nice," I said like I didn't mean it. "Well, that was a little close for comfort. That rock barely made it over our heads. How do we know he wasn't trying to hurt us like he did to that guy with the baseball bat?"

Willie's arm slid off my shoulder. He tugged on the brim of his hat, putting his face into shadow.

"Listen, Cassidy did a bad thing, no two ways about it.

But that guy was a big drunk, brought it on himself. It was at a summer league game and his son's team was losing. Cassidy hit a homer and then the next time he got up to bat this drunk dad stands up in the bleachers and yells at my boy, then throws a full beer can at him. Guy had a good arm—bounced right off Cassidy's helmet. He was only fourteen. He went after the guy, up into the bleachers with his bat. And for that, he did some time in juvie. Now he's just a motherless kid with an attitude problem."

I didn't know what to say. My mind winced at the images—the beer can bouncing off Cassidy's helmet, the bat swinging at the man's head. Willie took a deep breath, and let it out. "He was just trying to catch your attention, pard," he said. "Like I told your dad, just give him a chance. He doesn't mean any harm. He's just troubled, is all."

"Okay, if he leaves me alone, I'll give him a chance," I said. I stood up and walked over to Lisa with what was left of my sandwich.

"Hey," I said, as I sat down. Lisa didn't answer me, she just stared into the river, wiggling her brown feet around. I let my feet trail in the water beside hers.

"Willie was telling me about Cassidy—"

"I don't care. Cassidy's a creep."

"I thought you liked him."

"Can we like talk about something else?" She looked at me, her dark eyes full of sharp lights.

I didn't know what to say. I swallowed the last of my

sandwich. Then I said, "So why's your dad called Roger the Rogue?"

She shrugged. "'Cause after the army he moved up to southern Oregon and became a river rat, guiding raft trips down the Rogue River. Your dad came up from California to raft with him a couple of times when I was little. Stayed with us. They've been through a lot together."

"So your dad's a river rat, huh?"

"Oh yeah. His idea of a good time is living in the woods, in a tent, shooting rapids all the time. My idea of a good time is playing soccer, hanging out with my friends, listening to music and stuff."

"Me too, I guess." I said it but I wasn't sure I meant it. "And playing football," I added. "And I'm getting pretty good at skateboarding. But this is fun, too. I mean, like, sometimes. It's fun when it's fun."

"I know, right?" Lisa said. "If it weren't for that jerk whose name I won't mention."

"Yeah," I said. "Seems like he's got it in for us, big time. Well, me anyway. And my dad. Roger seems cool with him, though." I skimmed a stone across the river.

"My dad's cool with everybody. He used to be pretty wild himself. Another reason they call him 'Roger the Rogue.' So he doesn't get upset with anybody unless somebody actually gets hurt."

"Well, that could happen yet," I said. My upper teeth bit into my lower lip.

We fell silent for a moment, watching the river flow and spiral, like a snake shedding its skin. Then Lisa looked me up and down, and said, "Aren't you, like, too skinny for football?" She grinned, cocking one eyebrow.

"I'm not skinny—I'm *wiry!* And I'm stronger than you think."

"Well you went down pretty easy . . . for a *football* player!" She gave me a shove, which almost toppled me into the river.

"Geez! Watch it!" I sat back upright and said, "Yeah, well, you jumped me from behind . . . and the mud was slippery . . . and well . . . I slipped."

"I guess you 'slipped' again when I got you in a headlock and pinned you. Just like that." She snapped her fingers and grinned at me.

"Howdy. You two wanna come with me for a walk?" It was my dad. He was wearing cargo shorts, and it was embarrassing to look at his hairy, bony legs.

"Nah," I said. "We're good. We just wanna chill." I was actually starting to feel comfortable with Lisa, and now my dad had to come and ruin it.

"Come on, kiddo. Both of you. I want to show you some rock art. Old petroglyphs. It's not far."

I looked at Lisa. I could see she didn't want to go either, but we both shrugged, and I said, "I guess."

We hiked up this hot little side canyon, stepping between cactuses in our bare feet. We were in the badlands—dry gulches, dusty clumps of coyote brush, a ruin of boulders. More than once I thought I heard a tumble of stones behind us, but I didn't see anything.

"Watch out for snakes," Dad said. "Lots of rattlers around here." I glanced around, wishing I was wearing shoes. A minute later I saw something move next to the trail and I jumped about a foot, but it was just a harmless little whip-snake slithering under a rock.

Lisa bumped into me, like accidentally on purpose. I bumped her back. She gave me a wicked grin.

"Here we are, folks," Dad said, after a long hot walk. "Petroglyphs. Ancient rock art. They're carved into the rock, not painted."

"Cool," I said. There was a huge wall of pale, chiseled shapes against blackened rock. Pictures of bison, bighorn

sheep, elk or deer, coyotes . . . and way over to the right, some weird, triangular people-shapes with horns. And all around them there were these spirals and zigzags and what Dad called sunbursts.

"See, you guys," he said. "You can tell where ancient fires scorched it and smoke stained it. The Fremont Indians made these a long time ago. Way before the Utes moved into the area. Life here in the desert was precarious, dangerous. They tried growing corn, but the people here had to hunt in this desert to survive. Some say these petroglyphs were like prayers to draw the game to these canyons so the People could survive."

"Did they?" I asked.

"Did they what?"

"Survive."

"No. Not here, anyway. Life was a balancing act. The People had to balance the beauty and the terror. To stay in balance with nature. But maybe nature here was too harsh and they had to leave, or—"

"Look!" I said, jumping up onto a boulder. "I can balance!" I stood on one foot and balanced with my arms spread out like wings, my fingertips just brushing the petroglyph wall.

Lisa rolled her eyes at my lame attempt at humor.

"Get down, Aaron!" Dad barked. "And don't touch the wall! Wind and sand and time are doing enough damage without kids coming along with their grimy mitts and pawing the works."

"Geez, Dad, lighten up." I sat back down. "I was just . . . Whatever."

Dad, still in lecture mode, went on. "As I was saying, Aaron, the Fremont Indians left here over seven hundred years ago." He wiped the sweat from his forehead. "No one knows where they went. They may be the ancestors of the Utes, though. Utah was named after the Ute Indians. In fact, this whole stretch of Desolation Canyon is on the Ute reservation."

I'm actually interested in stuff like this, but sometimes my dad just drones on and on. Like now. But before he could continue his long-winded history lesson, I interrupted, "What are these squiggly lines? Snakes?"

"Looks like it."

I looked around. Lisa had wandered off, not exactly riveted by my dad's lecture.

"Watch where you step!" Dad called to her.

But it was too late.

Lisa shrieked. And then I heard it—the rapid, spooky rattle. Again. Then again.

Rattlesnake!

CHAPTER SEVEN

LITTLE ROCK HOUSE RAPIDS

F reeze, Lisa!" Dad yelled.

Lisa froze.

Then a rock ricocheted at Lisa's feet. She jumped back and Cassidy, out of nowhere, leaped down onto the trail and snatched something off the ground. It dangled from his hands.

The rattler! It was about six feet long and its head was smashed flat. I couldn't believe my eyes.

"You coulda got her killed, Cassidy!" Dad snapped, climbing over to Lisa and slipping an arm around her shoulders.

"What are you talking about, old man?" Cassidy growled. "I'm the one who saved her!"

"What if you'd missed? Did you think about that?" Dad shook his head. "Rattlers only attack if they're threatened. Leave 'em be and they'll leave you be. If you'd missed, it woulda struck her like lightning."

"But I didn't miss, did I?"

"Sometimes you got to think before you act," Dad said.

"Sometimes you got to act before someone gets bit!" Cassidy yelled back.

"Stop it!" Lisa said. My dad's shoulders drooped. She turned to Cassidy and said, "Thanks, Cass." It was the first time she ever called him "Cass." She even touched his arm as she said it.

I hated to admit it, but I was on Cassidy's side this time. He had killed the rattler, after all. But I couldn't help feeling useless and a little jealous. What had I done? Nothing. I froze at the sound of the deadly rattle. If Lisa was drowning in some rapids, would I jump in and try to save her? I wanted to think so, because I'm a strong swimmer. But rattlesnakes? I didn't know what to do. I just froze up.

"Well, thank goodness for your aim," Dad said. "If you'd been off by one inch . . . just one inch. . . ." He was shaking his head again, still angry.

Cassidy just scowled and held Dad's eyes, until Dad turned and started back down the trail. "Time to boogaloo down Broadway," he called over his shoulder. He said that to lighten the mood. He always said that and it always embarrassed me.

"Let's go," I said. We followed after Dad. Lisa glanced back over her shoulder at Cassidy.

I glanced back, too. But Cassidy stayed behind. He was firing rocks at the petroglyphs, sending sparks flying—and chips of cultural history. Good thing Dad didn't see him; he would have had a cow.

On the way back, I saw something scurry under a rock. Something way smaller than a snake. So I knelt and lifted the reddish rock. "A scorpion!" I said. Lisa's shadow fell over it. The scorpion's tail curled back, needle-sharp and vicious. I thought of smashing it with the rock, then thought, why not leave it alone? I carefully lowered the rock and stood up.

Lisa studied me, like she was trying to figure out a puzzle. "That was kinda cool, Aaron. Not killing the scorpion, I mean." Then she looked back over her shoulder, but Cassidy was nowhere in sight.

I think she was trying to tell me that being brave doesn't mean killing things for no reason.

But Cassidy had a reason. I think.

Dad asked me to help clean up and reload the kitchen boat. I'm lazy by nature, but I didn't mind. I wanted to be away from Cassidy, and I didn't even want to talk to Lisa. Not right now. I just wanted to think, and I could think and clean up at the same time.

Back home in California, I would boogie board in the ocean, or hop on my skim board in the sea foam, and I wasn't that afraid of getting hurt or drowning. I was in my element.

But out here in this canyon, with someone like Cassidy, I felt out of my element. Like I could be pulled in and drowned—or bit by a rattler. Or smashed by a boulder dropped by a sixteen-year-old with more tattoos on his body than teeth in his head. Or brain cells.

But how could I compete with him for Lisa's attention?

And what compelled me to even want to do that?

It seemed that two feelings were battling inside me: that I was better than Cassidy—smarter, more sensitive—and that I was inferior. Not as powerful. Not as brave.

But so what? I'm twelve and he's sixteen. Where's the level playing field in that? I should just be okay with who I am, right? Why is that so hard to do? I should like who I am and let Cassidy be who he is.

Or should I? He's totally unpredictable. You never know when he's trying to save a life or take a life. And he could be funny, which really drove me nuts. He was always making Lisa laugh. The only time I made her laugh was when she laughed *at* me.

Back home people actually think I'm funny. I'm kind of the class clown. Like one time I was sitting in the back of the class and cut up a poster with a pair of scissors until it dangled like a mobile, or piece of art. Then I held it up—right in the middle of a lecture by our teacher Mrs. Gruber—and said, "Will it sell?"

The class cracked up, and I had to go to the principal's office. Again.

But whenever I'm alone with girls, I get some kind of social brain freeze. Any attempts at humor go over like a deflating balloon.

"Earth calling Aaron," said Willie, snapping me out of my zone. "Why are you scrubbing the cheese?"

Back on the river we faced a strong headwind. I took turns with Dad at the oars—just like Lisa was doing with her dad. Against wind like that, it takes all your energy not to let the raft slip backwards.

Up ahead Cassidy was rowing the kitchen boat while his dad took a snooze. With a huge ice chest, a dutch oven, and all the food supplies, it was by far the heaviest raft, yet Cassidy was plowing ahead.

I switched again with Dad, and doubled my effort at the oars, inspired by Cassidy's example. If inspired is the right word for it.

That evening at camp, after chowing down on a great barbecued chicken dinner that Willie made, everybody just kicked back. Everybody except Cassidy, that is. He sat down in full lotus right in front of Lisa, then swung up into a handstand, his legs still crossed. Then he started walking around on his hands! Finally, he cartwheeled over and did three back flips—one, two, three—and crashed into the dark river with a big splash.

"Sweet!" Lisa cheered.

Not to be outdone, I jumped up and did a backward handspring—my one gymnastics move—and landed on my butt.

Lisa laughed. "You're so lame!"

I felt like a toad. I crawled to my tent and buried myself in my sleeping bag.

"That Cassidy," Dad said when he joined me, "is a show-off and out of control. And that's a dangerous combination."

I didn't say anything. I wrestled with my own mixed-up thoughts, while outside I could hear Cassidy running around howling like a coyote, free of self-doubt.

The next morning we were on the river by ten o'clock. I asked Roger if I could ride with him and Lisa, and he said yes. Lisa smiled and it made me feel good all over.

The river was swift here. Box elders and tamarack flicked by like light poles on the freeway. Swifts darted and spray flew. There wasn't a cloud in the sky.

We were coming up to Little Rock House Rapids. Roger said that with the high flow this year it could be a Class 3. Roger asked if I wanted to take over at the oars. "I think you can handle it, mate," he said when I looked at him doubtfully.

We switched places. "All right, now swing the raft around so you're facing forward and can read the river," Roger explained. Dad had been teaching me, but when it came to rapids, I still got butterflies in my stomach. "You want to find the main channel," he continued. "See that smooth tongue where the water current slides into a V-shape between the waves?" He pointed and I could see where he meant. "You want to aim right for the point of that V."

"Okay," I said through clenched teeth. I tugged at the oars and soon we slipped right into the V, as planned. The river was getting wilder and Roger had to shout so I could hear him.

"Now turn the raft around and pull hard!" he commanded. "You want to move the raft faster than the current, matey. That way you can control where it goes, instead of the current controlling you. Lisa will keep a lookout for boulders."

I braced my legs and rowed so hard that I practically stood up with each pull. While Lisa yelled warnings, I adjusted my aim and rowed even harder. We were swept bouncing down the rapids, wobbling and sliding over the boiling water and between boulders as big as little houses.

But when I looked back over my shoulder to check my position, there was a rock as big as a LARGE house.

And we were headed straight for it.

CHAPTER EIGHT

THE OUTLAW TRAIL

As we got closer I could see that it was really just a cliff wall jutting into the river. I pulled back into the main current and Lisa cheered as we shot out the other end of Little Rock House Rapids.

Or Not-So-Little Rock House Rapids, in my opinion. It was an epic ride.

I was speechless, but proud. Lisa was cheering *me*, not Cassidy. And man, did that feel good! *Sweet!*

"Good job, mate!" Roger said. I smiled, still speechless, my whole body shaking from more than the cold water soaking my skin.

Lisa took over at the oars. She smiled at me and warmth spread through my body again. I was probably blushing, but I doubt she could tell with my sunburn.

Soon we drifted down a quiet stretch of river. I glimpsed a fat catfish rising to the surface to nibble a dead dragonfly. I pointed it out to Lisa, but she wrinkled her nose. I noticed some mallards hiding in the cattails along the shore and shouted, "Hi, ducks!"

That's how good I felt.

Lisa laughed and said, "You're weird," but it seemed like she meant it in a good way.

I leaned back and looked up at the top edge of the canyon, towering high above us. Dad had said we were on the Tavaputs Plateau when we drove the twenty-five miles of bad road from the highway at the top of the plateau down to the put-in at Sand Wash. Up top we saw patches of evergreen forest and a small herd of Rocky Mountain elk, Utah's state animal, grazing in a meadow. (Dad told me the Shawnee Indians called them "wapiti," meaning "white rump.") But the lower we got, the drier and harsher the landscape got, and the fewer the wild animals we saw.

After a mile or so of silence, Roger launched into a lecture. Like my dad, he's full of information about everything . . . and always happy to share it. Sometimes it's interesting, but it can drive you crazy, too.

He took off his red bandanna, soaked it in the river, and tied it back on his head. Water dripped down his face as he told us how, back in 1869, Major John Wesley Powell became the first white man to paddle the Green River. The major wrote in his journal that this canyon was "a region of the wildest desolation." The name stuck.

"He rowed a wooden boat," Roger said, "and capsized it in Steer Ridge Rapids—which is coming up. And another time he smashed his boat to bits." He let that sink in for a while. It didn't add anything to my newfound, but still shaky confidence.

"This canyon was carved from ancient seas," he added. "In some places it's deeper than the Grand Canyon."

I looked up again. Massive walls soared to the sky, making me feel small and alone, yet somehow filled with a sense of hugeness. How could that be?

I didn't know.

We had a late lunch on a little pocket beach and I skipped a stone so well across the flat water that it almost reached the other side. Lisa didn't see it but Cassidy said, "Not bad. For an amateur."

He picked up a good skipping stone, probably about to show me who was the real pro, when Willie hollered, "Time to hit the road, folks!"

Cassidy fired his stone across the river, but no one saw it. I turned toward Lisa before it took its first skip.

I climbed back into Roger and Lisa's raft, after checking in with my dad to make sure it was okay with him. "As long as Roger doesn't mind, kiddo," he said. He told me how Roger had praised my handling of Little Rock House Rapids.

I beamed and said, "See ya, Dad," like maybe I wouldn't see him for a long time.

The river started picking up right away, through some

very dry country, mountains in the distance. Soon we came to Steer Ridge Rapids—what Roger called a "read and run" rapids, meaning we didn't have to stop to scout it out.

Roger rowed. Lisa was on the bow, keeping an eye out for trouble. "That's a nasty hole!" she shouted as we shot by it. I couldn't help remembering what Roger had said about Major Powell and his capsized boat, but this was just what my dad called a "wave-train": a fun bouncy ride down to smooth water again.

I sat in back and enjoyed the ride. *I could get used to this,* I thought.

Next was Jack Creek Rapids. Another "read and run" Class 3. Lots of big waves and a few deep holes. Lisa rowed this time and I called the shots from the bow. At the end we slapped high fives as we coasted into calm water.

Roger took over and soon we pulled over to check out Rock Creek Ranch, the ruins of an old homestead. Cassidy was already there, scouting around.

"Dude! What took you so long?" he asked when he saw me. But he turned away before I could think of a snappy answer.

Dad came in last, long after the rest of us. He looked a little haggard, but he gave me a big smile and a half-hug and said, "What's up, kiddo? How was it?"

"Awesome!" I answered. And I meant it.

We inspected a sagging log cabin, which had a couple of battered leather boots, lots of dusty antique bottles, and a

rusted potbelly stove. Rusty tools and iron traps still hung from the walls. It was pretty cool, making us feel like we were in the real Wild West.

It made me wonder who had lived down here in this lonesome place. Some homesteader dude.

Outside, there were sagging fences and old rusted farm equipment scattered around. And a few tree skeletons stood in what had once been an orchard, now gone wild. Roger started talking again.

"This ranch," he said, "and McPherson's downriver, were way stations for Butch Cassidy and the Wild Bunch. The Outlaw Trail ran right through here. The homesteaders sold fresh horses to the Wild Bunch when the posse was hot on their tail."

"So there's trails up out of here?" Cassidy asked, chewing on a weed.

"If you can find 'em," Roger said. He peered up toward the cliff top. "But you wouldn't make it far, mate. This here's some of the wildest country in the West. Rattlers, scorpions, mountain lions. And the ghosts of the Wild Bunch haunting the dry gulches." Deep laugh lines creased Roger's face.

Cassidy spat and walked off, kicking up dust with his Doc Martens. I watched Lisa watching him go. Then she turned to me and jabbed a sharp elbow into my ribs.

"Geez!" I jumped back and rubbed my ribs.

"You think Cassidy's haunted by the ghosts of the Wild Bunch?" she asked.

"I think he's haunted by bashing a man in the head with a baseball bat." It was out of my mouth before I could stop it. Great, me trying to be funny again.

Sure enough, Lisa didn't laugh. "I think his mind's elsewhere," she said.

I kicked a dirt clod and didn't know what to say.

I went and laid down in the shade of a gnarly orchard tree and tried to take a nap. I might've snoozed a little—I saw visions of a posse riding in a cloud of dust, like from an old Hollywood Western—but I kept waking up.

Tension in the air.

Tension in my stomach.

A half hour later, Cassidy still wasn't back.

Roger, and then my dad, started calling his name. It was time to go. It was past time to go, actually.

"Why don't you just leave him alone?" Lisa told them. "Give him a little space to calm down. He's a teenager. Remember when you were a teenager, Dad?"

"It's time to hoist the anchors, lassie," Roger said with a grin.

"CA-A-A-S-S-S-I-I-D-D-YYY!" roared Wild Man Willie. Only his name echoed back.

"We won't make it to our next camp spot by dark if we don't skedaddle now," Dad said. His bony face tensed in the cliff shadows.

"That darn kid," said Willie, flapping dust off his pants with his felt hat.

"I'll look for him, mate," Roger said.

"We'll all look for him," Dad said.

Except for Lisa, we all fanned out in the direction of the cliffs and started searching for Cassidy, calling his name over and over. I looked back. Lisa leaned against a fence-post, hugging herself.

It was getting dark. A shadow fell over us as the sun disappeared beyond the ridge. A chill wind blew down the canyon, and, for some reason, my heart clenched like a fist.

CHAPTER NINE

WATER BABIES

CA-A-A-S-S-S-I-I-D-D-YYY!" Willie howled again.

And again only his name echoed back. We'd been looking for him for about half an hour. Our little side-canyon had grown dark and cold, and everybody was getting restless and a little scared and angry. Even Lisa.

Willie was about to throw his hat into the river when we heard what sounded like a coyote. But the closer it got, the better we could hear it:

"YIPPY-KI-YAY! YIPPY-KI-YO!"

And here came Cassidy, whistling like he didn't have a care in the world.

"Where the devil have you been?" growled Willie.

"We were about to send a posse out after you!" Roger said, trying to make a joke of it. But nobody was laughing.

"It's no joke," Dad said. "Sign's posted, we can't camp here. And the next good spot is about two miles downriver—and we've lost the sun. Come on, man," he said to Cassidy, "no more dilly-dallying. We can't always

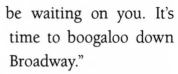

be waiting on you. It's time to boogaloo down Broadway."

Cassidy walked right up to Dad, glared at him, and said, "I'll boogaloo YOU down Broadway, dude."

"Cassidy, get your rear in gear," Willie growled.

"Then get this skinny old man outta my face!" Cassidy spat. "If he wasn't so slow at the oars, we'da been here and gone an hour ago. I was just checking out this sweet little canyon to see if I could find the Outlaw Trail. . . ."

"Cassidy!" Willie cut in. "Zip it! We'll talk about this later. Time waits for no man."

I was getting bent out of shape by Cassidy all over again. Did he think the whole world revolved around him? *Geez!*

By the time we got back in the boats, it was late dusk and it was getting dark fast. I thought about what Cassidy had said. Dad was kind of slow at the oars. But still, Cassidy shouldn't have talked to him like that. It just added to the tension. We should be having fun, right? Not fighting about everything.

An owl flew low overhead. White-ish, like a ghost. Maybe a barn owl. I read in a book somewhere that some people believe when an owl hoots or flies over you it means some-body's going to die.

Great.

We finally pulled into a good camp spot as the first stars poked out in the narrow sky above the canyon. We hauled up our rafts and had to use our flashlights to unload, lug our gear to a flat spot in the trees, and set up our tents.

We didn't speak. No one spoke. Each person had their own thoughts and their own chores. There was wood to be gathered, a fire to be made, food to be prepped.

After a tasty dinner of meat pies with peas and potatoes, we sat around the fire sipping hot cocoa and telling jokes. Everyone but Cassidy and my dad, that is. Cassidy had stalked off into the dark, and Dad sat alone by the river, looking up at the stars. The sky was thick with them now, and they flashed sharp and bright in the crystal air.

Dad was a stargazer. He could tell you more than you needed to know about the constellations.

"Hey, Dad," I said, feeling kind of sorry for him because of how Cassidy had talked to him. Dad could be pretty annoying, but he could be fun sometimes, too.

And anyway, he was my dad.

"What's up, kiddo?"

"Want some hot cocoa?"

Dad shrugged. The river flowed by, mirroring the Milky Way.

We sat silently together for a few more minutes, then Dad got up and moved to a stump by the fire. I followed and Roger handed him a steaming cup of cocoa.

"It's a good night for scary stories," Roger said.

"Just so happens I know one, too." Dad said.

"Well then, mate, let's hear it!"

Dad stared into his mug for a while, as if he were waiting for it to tell him the story. "Well," said Dad, "it's an old Ute story. This is Indian country, you know. Has been for over a thousand years. First the Fremonts, then the Utes."

"Just tell the story, Dad!" I said. Sometimes he drove me crazy!

We all huddled closer to the fire. The shadows seemed to bend and huddle with us.

"Well," Dad said, "it's about the water babies."

"What are water babies?" I asked.

Dad sipped his hot cocoa and stroked his beard. "It's kind of spooky," he said, looking around at each of us. "Sure you want to hear it?"

"Yes!" I blurted, way too loud. I scooted back next to the river; the heat of the fire made my sunburned face sting even more than it already did.

"Long ago," Dad said, pausing to sip his cocoa again, "the People were troubled, they were scared. Men kept disappearing. They'd go off on a hunting trip along the river—this river here—but they wouldn't come back." Dad put down his mug and warmed his hands over the fire.

"Now every once in a while," he said, "a hunter would come back after a long absence, but he'd be talking crazy. He'd babble and carry on and pull his hair, and the only thing you could understand was something about the water babies.

'It's the water babies!' the crazy one would say. 'In the river!' And he'd babble on and on like the sound of the river itself."

Dad paused. The river babbled.

"Then what happened?" Lisa asked. She was shivering, and I wanted to slip my arm around her, but didn't dare. In the fire, dying flames leaped like ghosts and disappeared into the night.

"Now the water babies," Dad continued, "were tiny creatures, about the size of a man's hand." He spoke so quietly we all had to lean closer to hear him.

"They had long black hair, longer than their bodies," he said. "Their demented cries would make your blood boil."

He plucked the hawk feather from his hatband and used the tip of it to pick his teeth. Gross! Then he ran his tongue over his teeth and stuck the feather back in his hatband, and continued.

"The water babies lived in the river, and when a hunter came too close—to spear a fish or get a drink—the water babies would leap up and scream! They were tiny, but insanely powerful. They'd screech like something from another world, then reach out and pull the hunter down, down, down into the river and drown him."

"Aaaaiiiiiyaaaahhhh!"

A scream pierced the night, stopping my heart. Everyone went silent, frozen in fear. Then a hand grabbed my ankle with supernatural strength and dragged me, kicking and screaming, into the icy river.

Of course, I knew it had to be Cassidy. But I felt like I was drowning anyway. I gulped water as I twisted and kicked, but the more I fought the worse I made it. I was being dragged down further and further under the water. My lungs screamed for air.

I knew he'd let me go. Any time now. This was just another one of his "practical jokes," as Willie had called them.

But I wondered if Cassidy knew how long I could hold my breath.

CHAPTER TEN

THE BLUE SKY PEOPLE

At last he let go and I shot to the surface.

And inhaled half the night sky.

"CASSIDY!" I gasped.

And there he was. Flopping around in the shallows, clutching his belly and laughing.

Everybody was laughing, except me and my dad. I must have been a funny sight, but I was too shook up to laugh, and too embarrassed. I crawled out and rolled on my back in the sand, coughing up river water and trying to catch my breath.

"Cassidy, you're too much for me," Dad said as he stood up and headed for our tent.

"Dude! Lighten up! Chill, man!" Cassidy stripped off his soaking T-shirt and snapped it at Dad's back, missing by inches.

The laughter stopped—except for Cassidy's.

"Cassidy," Willie said, low and quiet. A warning, I guess. But Willie still had half a grin on his face. Sometimes he acted more like a big brother to his son than a father. But like Dad said, Cassidy's a handful and Willie's a single parent. What can you do with a kid that crazy?

Still, the image of him snapping his T-shirt like a towel at Dad's backside. It was so . . . disrespectful, so aggressive, it made my stomach hurt.

Cassidy, still chuckling, flung his shirt over a branch and squatted next to the fire. I climbed to my feet, dripping, and sat as far away from him as I could and still feel the heat of the coals. I rubbed the goose bumps on my arms. Nobody said anything, we just sat and listened to the river muttering in its dark bed.

It was hard to sleep. I tried to talk to Dad, but he still wasn't talking.

"Sorry, Dad," I said. I kept trying to erase the image of Cassidy snapping his wet T-shirt at my dad, like some bully in the locker room.

Dad was a storyteller. Maybe he could make a story out of all this.

Or maybe I could, someday.

To sleep, I thought of Lisa instead of Cassidy. But it didn't help. I tossed and turned until I finally drifted off, like a broken branch floating down the Green River.

In the morning I woke to a loud clang.

I rubbed my eyes and looked around. Dad was gone. I lifted the tent flap and squinted out into the early morning sun as it burst through a V-notch in the lip of the canyon. A lizard scurried beneath a rock. Otherwise, nothing moved in the white glare.

Then I heard voices. Loud voices. I crawled out of the tent, then tiptoed toward the kitchen area.

Cassidy held a long-handled black skillet in his hand. His muscles bulged and twisted like ropes. Dad stood facing him, one foot on a big fallen limb.

"I'm getting tired of your attitude, Cassidy," Dad said. "Your bad attitude."

"Dude! I said get out of my face!"

"It's time to talk this out," Dad said, barely controlling his anger.

"Back off!" Cassidy banged the pan against the trunk of a tree. I jumped involuntarily.

"You and your practical jokes," Dad said. "Or are they jokes? You throw rocks at people, almost get Lisa bit by a snake, practically drown Aaron last night and—"

"Yeah, dude," Cassidy cut in, "and I wish it was you. I woulda drowned your skinny—"

"Hey hey hey hey!" barked Willie. He was crawling out of his tent. "Sounds like a coupla roosters had a bad night. Cassidy? How many times do I have to tell ya to zip it?"

Roger shuffled over, scratching his grizzled face. "Where's the coffee? Hot java to cool down them early morning river jitters," he said, and kicked the dead coals from last night's fire. Everybody was up now, except for Lisa.

"Me and Cassidy are just having a little chat about—"

"Bull!" shouted Cassidy. "This jackass has been on my case ever since we hit the river! Who made him the boss man? He ain't the law! " He clanged the pan one more time, then let it drop to the ground with a bang.

"*Cassidy!*" This time Willie boomed. He was clenching his fists and his face was turning red.

Then I saw Lisa. She was half-hiding behind the cottonwood tree. In the leaf shadows she looked like a tree nymph from a fairy tale. I nodded, but she didn't seem to notice. She just brushed the black hair from her dark eyes and stared intently at Cassidy's every move.

"Let's brew us some coffee—" Roger started to say, but Cassidy cut him off with a machine-gun blast of swearwords.

"Cool it!" Willie snapped. He was getting mad now. Really mad.

"This could be a fun trip—" Dad started to say.

"Yeah, crazy mad fun," Cassidy interrupted, "if you weren't here to ruin it!"

"Dropping rocks on people's heads is your idea of fun? Half-drowning them as a joke?"

"No, dude, rowing in slow mo' and acting like a jerk—!"

"Kids! Kids!" Roger cut in. He tried to laugh, but there was nothing to laugh about.

"This isn't a joke!" Dad said, his eyes hard as stones.

"Dude! You're the joke!" Cassidy pointed at Dad. "Ha-ha!"

"And you're a joker with an attitude!" Dad retorted. "A real macho man. All bravado and he-man antics, like a phony TV wrestler."

"Stand down, guys! Both of you!" Willie snapped. "You're both out of line!"

Veins popped out in Cassidy's neck. He looked like he was going to explode.

Dad just stood there trembling like a skinny river willow in a strong breeze. Willie came around the camp table toward them.

Too late.

In one swift movement, Cassidy faked left, then ducked and lifted one end of the limb Dad was half-standing on, up-ending him into the sand.

Dad landed with a thunk. "Are you crazy?" he yelped.

Cassidy couldn't speak. Words seemed to press at his clenched lips to get out, and his face twisted with a dark, crazy anger. His eyes bulged into hard bullets as he knelt and wrestled the big limb up onto his shoulders. Then he stood and jerked it up over his head, beads of sweat popping out on his forehead.

Lisa screamed, *"Cassidy!"* just as Willie lunged toward him.

Dad rolled away just as Cassidy let out a blood-curdling yell that made the hair on my head stand up. I was shaking, unable to think or do anything.

Willie leaped between Cassidy and my dad.

Cassidy froze. His eyes darted around and snagged on Lisa. Suddenly all the pent-up hate and anger seemed to drain out of him. Maybe he realized, finally, what he was doing. He dropped the limb in the sand and ran off.

The fist that was my heart unclenched and it felt like the first pure air in a long time filled my lungs. I let it out slowly.

"Go soak your head in the river, Cassidy!" Willie shouted. "And cool off."

Dad climbed to his feet and dusted off his legs. He rubbed his hip and stretched his back. He looked shook-up, haggard, hollowed out. He stooped over and picked up his fallen hat, dusted it off, and placed it gingerly back on his head.

"I could sure use a cup of coffee," he said.

We broke camp like zombies, going slowly through the motions. The sound of the river came back, along with the sound of the birds. All had seemed to fall to silence, watching the one-sided fight in the sand. The overgrown man-boy bursting with some kind of dark rage that even he couldn't understand. Nobody could understand. And the daunted, angry man rolling in the sand. My dad. Unable to do anything about it.

We rowed till noon, all floating on our separate islands. Dad and I didn't speak. I could see his mind was far away. We took turns at the oars and I tried to take my mind off things by looking for river otters and eagles and mountain lions along the high cliffs. Roger had said there were black bears in the hills, but we hadn't seen any yet. I did see some large birds circling atop the thermals, but I couldn't tell for sure if they were eagles or vultures.

During lunch Roger tried to ease the tensions by telling a Ute creation story. Dad, who loves these stories and knows many, said he wasn't hungry and walked off on his own. Cassidy peered after him and spat in the sand.

But Roger, after mopping his face with his bandanna, continued. "First, I wanna say that the name *Ute* comes from *Yutta*, the Blue Sky People. That's what the other tribes called 'em. They called themselves *Nuche*, the People."

"Just tell the story, Dad," Lisa complained. Cassidy flicked a piece of bark at her, and grinned. She threw it back, staring daggers at him. "But shorter, okay?"

Roger looked around to see if my dad was coming back. Cassidy rolled onto his back with a sigh, and flopped his arms out, as if we were being crucified by the sky.

"Okay," Roger said. He pulled his bandanna back around his head and took a sip from his canteen. "In the beginning, as the story goes, the earth was flat. Flat as my hand." He held his hand palm up. "The Creator told Hawk to make a target. When Hawk had done what he was told, Creator notched an arrow in his bow and drew back on the bowstring. He pulled back with so much force that when he released the arrow, it glanced off Hawk's target and plowed through the desert, gouging out deep gorges. And that, according to the Blue Sky People, is how Desolation Canyon came to be."

Willie started to say something but Dad was coming back and everybody grew quiet. Cassidy sat up and pulled back on an imaginary bow. Closing one eye, he took aim at my dad and released the imaginary arrow.

"Pow! You're dead."

CHAPTER ELEVEN

THE DISAPPEARANCE

That night Dad said he wanted to sleep out alone under the stars. Cassidy asked Lisa if she wanted to play cards, but she said no. We all went our separate ways. I wrote in my journal, but just about the canyon and the river, and what we had for dinner. Nothing about what was really going on, underneath.

When I finally drifted off to sleep, Cassidy invaded my dreams. They swirled with the drama that seemed to be engulfing us all and pulling us down—like the raging river itself, or the Water Babies in the story.

I woke in the middle of the night to what I thought was a loud crash. At some earlier point Dad had crawled back into our tent and was snoring away. When I looked out the tent flap, mine was the only head sticking out.

I looked around. I saw a large dark shape, darker than the night. It was huge and hunched over, like a bear. Like a black bear.

But it wasn't moving. Was it just a boulder? Had I just been dreaming that I'd heard a loud crash?

I clapped my hands to see if the black shape moved, but it didn't, and the only growls I heard were the ones Dad was making. Must be a boulder.

The next day the headwind hit us early and Dad and I had to sit facing each other, doubled up on the oars—him pulling, me pushing. My mind kept replaying images from yesterday—Cassidy hoisting the heavy limb, my dad sprawled in the sand, Lisa hiding behind a tree—and I wanted to say something, but we were straining so hard at the oars that we couldn't speak.

Even doubled up, we moved turtle-slow in that wind, and by lunchtime the other two rafts were far out of sight ahead of us. By the time we got to the pull-out, the others had already eaten lunch and were ready to head out again.

"Change of plans!" Cassidy said, hopping onto the bow of our raft. "Dude," he said to me, "join Roger. I'm rowing this rig. Your dad's holding up the show, big time."

This struck me as a dangerous mix—like fire and gunpowder—but Dad just pulled his hat down tight and said grimly, "Okey-dokey. Aaron, go on and help Roger out, okay, kiddo?"

I looked at him, my eyes pleading, *Are you nuts?* He just nodded. I snatched my gear and jumped ashore. Willie handed me a sandwich wrapped in foil and tossed one to

Dad. I untied Roger's raft and helped push it out, then Lisa and I hopped in together. I was going to help Roger row but Lisa got there before me.

Roger tossed me a bag of gorp (my favorite mix of nuts and chocolate) and said, "Your dad and Cassidy have some issues to work out, mate."

I guess Roger still didn't see Cassidy as a dangerous problem for all of us—at least, he wasn't showing it if he did.

Willie looked at Cassidy and my dad, shook his head, then untied the kitchen raft, gave it a shove, and hopped in. He was going solo.

The wind got worse and worse. It roared down the canyon like a locomotive. It got so strong it actually started to push the river back upstream, blowing us backwards with each gust. The wind created waves that were five feet high and some gusts lifted the front of our raft clear into the air.

"Gusts like this can flip a boat like a pancake," Roger yelled. I had to sit in the bow just to hold it down, hanging on for dear life. Roger and Lisa rowed. I offered to spell her but she just shook her head and kept rowing, harder than ever.

The last I saw of Dad's boat, Cassidy was alone at the oars, his muscles bulging, his cap turned backwards. Guess he wouldn't let Dad help him. Even without doubling up at the oars, he'd pulled about fifty yards ahead of the rest of us. Pretty soon they were out of sight around the next bend.

I was drenched from the spray and freezing cold when Lisa finally let me spell her at the oars, opposite

Roger. I rowed with all I had, and in no time I was dog-tired, too. But I wasn't about to show it. I rowed stroke for stroke with Roger, but between strokes we slipped backwards in the wind.

Finally Roger signaled Willie to eddy out. *Thank God*, I said to myself. We could rest where the current turned back on itself and died along the shore.

"Gotta hold up till the wind drops!" Roger yelled. The wind tore his words away. Sand crusted his lips. He looked as wild and grizzled as a pirate.

We lashed our boats together and hunkered down in the eddy next to shore. Our rafts sloshed around and bumped with each gust of wind.

For an hour, maybe two, we stayed huddled like that, shivering with the cold. My right arm and knee were pressed against Lisa's, though, and that at least kept my heart warm.

Any attempt at talking and the words were ripped from our mouths. I thought of whispering something cool in Lisa's ears, but I couldn't think of anything.

Suddenly the wind scurried something upriver toward us. It skimmed the surface, dancing across waves, and flipped over next to our raft.

"Dad's hat!" I yelled, fishing it out. The crown of his straw hat was crushed and stained a dark maroon. The feather was missing.

"Blood," Roger said, taking the hat from my hand and staring at it.

My mind froze. My heart thundered. Roger stuffed Dad's hat beneath a strap, and said, "Let's move it! *Go go go go!*"

Ropes flew and everybody scrambled to their places.

I helped Roger row and Lisa held down the bow. We battled the wind but the current was faster now so we made better time. Plus adrenalin surged through me, flushing fatigue from my veins and sending shots of pure energy to my heart.

We rowed and rowed, carving the water, curving through canyons of red sand. Still no sign of Dad's boat.

Nothing.

Panic gnawed at me like a rat. Suddenly I leaped up and traded places with Lisa in the bow as we rounded the bend and there it was.

Their raft!

It was upside down, half out of the water on the sandy beach.

Dad and Cassidy were gone. My heart hung suspended

in a high dive off a steep cliff. My eyes, like caged animals, searched the shore.

"Dad! Dad!" I screamed against the wind and the water and the cliffs.

Once ashore it took all of us to heave Dad's raft over, right-side up. It was like wrestling a giant kite in that wind.

Inside, more blood. Splattered all over. It felt like a knee to my gut.

"Oh my God!" Lisa cried.

My mind was still frozen. I searched frantically, expecting to see my dad, expecting to hear him say, "What's up, kiddo?"

"Tracks," Willie called out. He was kneeling in the moist sand nearby and we all knelt beside him. "Cassidy's," he said, pointing. The wind had smeared the tracks; to me they were barely visible.

"How do you know?" I asked, my voice cracking.

"Cassidy's Doc Martens," he said. "The tread is pretty obvious. Your dad was wearing river sandals."

Cassidy's boot tracks led up the beach, then into the brush toward the high canyon walls.

Alone.

CHAPTER TWELVE

THE SEARCH

I was frantic. I started running up and down the beach, looking for Dad, calling his name. "Dad! Dad!"

"Aaron! It's getting dark fast," Willie said, trying to calm me down. "I'm going to follow Cassidy's tracks while there's still light. You stick with Roger. He wants to get camp set up so there's a warm place to bring Cassidy and your dad back to, once we find them."

Willie had been a squad leader in the Iraqi desert, so I figured he knew what he was doing. He was following the tracks of his only son, but I couldn't think about that right now.

Dad was my only dad.

I started jogging along the river again. Roger called after me but I kept running, hopping over rocks, looking into the river, scanning the shoreline.

But soon the cliff walls came straight down into the water, blocking my way. I shouted Dad's name one more time, kicked the sand, and turned back. Still running.

We managed to set up camp quickly in among the rocks and tamarisk bushes. Roger said I could lie down and rest while he and Lisa set up, but there was no way that was an option. I didn't want to think; I wanted to keep moving. I wanted to look for Dad, but there was stuff to get done. Lisa stayed by my side; she even helped me pitch our tent—Dad's and mine.

Dad.

The word lodged in my throat like a stone. I had to keep working, keep busy. But my eyes kept darting around, searching, searching. Maybe I'd see a clue.

Roger said, "Stay put, mate," and scouted along the river, wading hip high where the cliffs met the water. I started to go after him, but I wasn't sure I could handle what we might find. I fought off the image of Dad's dead and shredded body, and after slipping on a mossy rock, I finally turned back.

Lisa was right behind me. "Come on, Lisa. Let's get some wood. Make a fire. Maybe my dad will see it." It was wishful thinking, but it was almost full dark now.

"I'm sorry," Lisa said, touching my arm. I pulled away and scrambled over boulders, scrounging for driftwood.

I saw a movement across the river—something dark slithering into water. I kept looking, but it was gone. Probably a mink or river otter.

Lisa and I collected a big pile of wood—enough to last all night—and took turns chopping some of the larger pieces with an ax. When it was my turn, I drove the ax into the wood with so much fury that Lisa said, "Stop it, Aaron. You want to lose your leg?"

Better than losing a dad, I thought, but didn't say.

Roger came back, slipping on wet boulders. He was soaking wet, and he looked worn out.

"Sorry, Aaron," he said. Everybody was sorry. My dad was gone, just slipped into darkness like the mink or otter, and everybody was sorry.

What could have happened? Did the boat flip and he . . . drowned? I couldn't even say the word to myself. Or did Cassidy clobber him with an oar, like the man he hit with the bat?

And if Dad went under, why did Cassidy take off on his own? Wouldn't he have tried to save him?

I waved my hands in front of my face, swatting away images like flies. I had no tears. Not yet, anyway. I lurched forward and snatched up a long piece of driftwood.

We got a fire going. Roger changed into dry clothes, then sat on a stump and unfolded a big map of Desolation Canyon. The wind had died down to a deadly stillness, but the map shook in Roger's hands.

We heard a shout. I jumped up, heart pounding in my throat.

But it was only Willie. Alone. He threw his hat on the ground and squatted by the fire. He was breathing hard.

"It got too dark to look anymore. And the wind, it wiped out most of Cassidy's tracks. I climbed as far as I could, then had to turn around." He rubbed his eyes and a wrinkle shaped like a bird's wings creased his forehead. A tremor passed through him. He picked up his hat, put it on, took it off again, then slapped it back on.

"According to the map," Roger said, "there's a side canyon back in there that looks like it might lead up to the rim."

"Yeah, I saw a trail of sorts," Willie said, "but it looked more like a deer path to me. It might just lead into a box canyon, a dead end. Or—who knows—it could wind its way on up to the top. We'll climb it first thing in the morning."

"The Outlaw Trail," I said. I tried to laugh, but nothing was funny. Silence, filled with the roar of the river, the roar of my heart. Were they all thinking what I was thinking? Cassidy the outlaw. Dad probably tried to help him row, got up in his face, so Cassidy whacked him with an oar, blood flying. Why else would Cassidy run away? He was fleeing the scene of the crime.

"I think the raft flipped in the wind," Willie said, as if he read my mind and wanted to stand up for his son.

"Then why'd Cassidy run?" I spat it out. Somebody had to say it.

Nobody answered. Everybody stared at the fire.

All of a sudden the night sky crushed down on me. I turned away from the fire and clutched my head.

Then Lisa was sitting beside me and slipped her arm around me. I started to rock and she rocked with me.

Still no tears. My head felt like a stone under tremendous

pressure. A stone about to burst into a million pieces, a million shards.

Willie jumped up and let out a howl like a coyote. Like Cassidy. Was he hoping to hear Cassidy howl back, or was it a howl of despair?

Roger got up and walked Willie a few feet away from the fire. He put his arm around Willie's shoulder and bent close.

"If he fell in the river," Roger whispered, "his body would have risen to the surface after a while. It would have floated downriver and eddied out, or got caught by a snag." He must have thought I couldn't hear him, but I could hear every word as it bit into my flesh like a monster horsefly. "I would have found him," Roger said.

"Not if the river took him, pard," Willie whispered back. "His body could have got stuck in a keeper hole."

I sat up with a jolt and asked, "What's a keeper hole?" I was flooded with dread.

"Just rest, mate," Roger said. "Lisa, maybe you could help him to his tent, sweetheart?"

I jumped to my feet. "I don't want to rest! I want to know what a keeper hole is! I want my dad back!"

Roger stared at me. He knew I wasn't going to let this go. I hadn't seen him crying, but his eyes were red as if he had.

Finally he answered, "A keeper hole's a whirlpool eddy that sucks you down and holds you under. You could circle around and round down there forever."

"*Geez!* So you're gonna leave my dad there, spinning round and round forever?" I was getting dizzy, nauseous. It felt like a swirling, dark hole was funneling me down, down, like in the nightmare I'd had on our first night.

"Now listen up, son," Willie said. "Here's what we're gonna do. We're gonna wait here tonight for your dad and Cassidy. All of us. Together. That path I saw back there may or may not lead up to the rim, but we don't have time to find out. We don't know jack about what happened. I'm sure your dad's alive. He probably floated downriver and right now he's holed up in a cave, trying to keep warm. Maybe Cassidy climbed up out of the canyon to signal a plane for help. If he did, he's gonna need help himself. It's total desert up there and he'll be wanting for water. Or maybe he ran into a box canyon and is heading back down now. Just in case, when we leave tomorrow, we'll leave your dad's raft behind. But tonight we wait. Tomorrow we search down-river and try to get help. That's the plan. Nobody's dead 'til the fat lady sings."

The fat lady? Who's the fat lady?

All I could see were flowers of blood blooming on the raft. And a keeper hole with a skeleton whirling around inside. Dad's skeleton.

I rammed my fists into my eye sockets. I had to get rid of these images.

I had to think.

No, I couldn't think. Not straight thoughts, anyway.

"AAAAAAAHHHHHHHHHH!" I just had to yell or I would explode.

I stalked toward the river. I'm not sure what I was going to do. Maybe jump in, just to drown out the images. The deadly anxious fear. The feeling of doom.

Then I heard a sound and I stopped to listen. It was coming from way up the canyon walls, up where the stars choked the narrow sky.

It sounded like the yipping of a coyote.

Or my dad, calling my name.

CHAPTER THIRTEEN

THE NIGHTMARE

I kept listening . . . but there was nothing more. Just the river-speak of the canyon and the hiss of the fire.

And the dread.

"Musta been coyotes," Roger said.

Or Cassidy, with his coyote howl, I thought. But I didn't say anything. What was there to say?

"I'll rustle up some grub," Willie said. "We got to eat." He tossed a chunk of wood into the fire and clambered off to fetch the food chest.

"We have to find my dad!" I snapped back.

"We will, son. We will. Tomorrow. It's too dark now. The last thing we need is another lost person on this trip."

Willie marched off. I stared after him. I couldn't think. I took a step into the darkness and almost fell. I stopped and swayed in the darkness.

I felt like a caged animal.

I didn't think I could eat, so I staggered off toward my tent.

"I'll go with you," Lisa said, reaching out and touching my arm. I kept walking.

I crawled into my sleeping bag fully clothed. Lisa sat at the opening of my tent. "Do you want me to come in?" she asked. It was almost a whisper.

I didn't answer. Yes, I wanted her to come in, but I couldn't say it. I could barely even think it.

She got up and walked away. *Great*, I thought. *My dad's missing. Maybe dead. And just when I don't want Lisa to go, she goes.*

Then she was back. "I brought you something to eat. You should eat something."

She reminded me of my mother. But not really. Mom was always saying, "Eat your dinner, pumpkinseed. You have to eat. You're a growing boy."

But Lisa didn't sound like my mom. Lisa was nothing like my mom, actually. Except they both could be sweet.

Lisa knelt at the entrance holding something that smelled good. Real good. But my stomach was churning and twisting. I couldn't eat. I knew I couldn't eat.

"Eat," she said again.

She held out a bowl of soup. Chicken soup, from the smell of it. Steam rose in the tent and curled around me.

"I can't," I said.

I was hungry, I think. It was hard to tell. My stomach twisted and made weird gurgling sounds. But I could not eat.

"I could feed you," she said, a tiny smile hesitating on her lips.

Was that flirting in her voice? Now?

"I can spoon the soup into your mouth like I did when my grandma had pneumonia."

Flirting or not, I wasn't in the mood.

"I'm not your grandmother! And I can't eat right now, so knock it off!"

Her face crumpled and she looked like she might cry. But instead she said, "I feel like throwing this at you." They were angry words, but she didn't sound angry. Just sad.

"Why don't you?" I answered. "I wouldn't feel a thing." And it was true. Except for my stomach, I felt totally numb. My body. My tongue. "I think I'm . . ."

All of a sudden the words just drained out of me, like the last of the sand in an hourglass.

Lisa set down the bowl of soup and crawled into my tent. She sat cross-legged beside me, her head hunched beneath the slope of the tent wall. I could smell her. Coconut. Maybe she washed her hair with coconut shampoo.

I didn't know what to say, and even if I did, I doubt I could've said it. I really liked her being there, but I couldn't tell her that. No way. I closed my eyes, as if that would help me, protect me.

"Your dad'll be okay," she said. But it was just something people say. It didn't help.

"You'll see," she said, after a long pause. "Like one time when our cat, Mango, went missing. She was an orange cat, almost blind. She was gone for a whole week, and we thought she was dead for sure. Then one day she just showed up, like nothing had happened."

He left no footprints! I wanted to shout at her. *He went into the river and he didn't come back! He could be dead. And he's not a cat—he's my DAD!*

Lisa kept talking, but I couldn't hear her anymore. My thoughts raced along, tumbling down rapids, bouncing off boulders, dunking under the water, then kicking back up toward the surface again, screaming for air.

Finally, I drifted off to sleep. I dreamt that we were in our raft—me and Dad—rolling over the edge of a bottomless waterfall. I panicked and clawed the air, but suddenly the dream changed. I was in a tunnel. A long, dark tunnel. Alone. There was no light at the other end. Water dripped, making hollow plops, but there was no other sound.

I stepped forward cautiously, blindly, splashing through rank shallow water.

Squirmy things touched my legs. Swished and gurgled and plunged. Then rose to the surface.

Water babies!

They snatched at me. I tumbled in. I was sinking. I was sliding under. I thought I was awake and couldn't sleep but really I was asleep, dreaming I was awake, sinking into a deep, watery grave.

Suddenly, the dream switched again and I was spinning around and around underwater, funneling down. A trickle of water tickled my throat and I started to cough. To gag. To panic.

In the middle of my frenzied fight for life, I heard a sound.

Dad!

I stopped struggling and listened. Dad was calling me from far away, in the dark, beyond the water.

"A-a-a-a-a-r-r-o-n-n! A-a-a-a-a-r-r-o-n-n!"

CHAPTER FOURTEEN

CANYON SPIRITS

I sat bolt upright. It was no dream! Lisa was curled up beside me, outside my sleeping bag. She was sleeping, clutching herself in a hug.

"It's my dad!" I shouted.

Lisa jerked awake. "Did you hear something?" she said.

She didn't wait for an answer. She threw back the tent flap and we scrambled out into the darkness together. The bowl of soup toppled over. We looked up and above us the night was a river of stars between the canyon walls.

I heard noises and saw two dark figures dart from the other tents. Our camp was suddenly a hive of activity.

One of the dark forms came close. It was Willie, wild-eyed.

"Follow me," he said. *"Now!"*

I ducked back into my tent, grabbed my flashlight, and followed.

Willie joined Roger, who was carrying a first aid kit

under his arm, and the two of them lead the way up toward the dark looming cliffs.

Willie stopped, drew his hunting knife, and cut a branch off some brush. "Creosote," he said. "Makes a great torch." With a flick of his lighter, he set it aflame.

Soon we were climbing a steep and windy deer path by the light of a torch.

This was really happening. It felt like I was in another dream, but it wasn't a dream. It was real. I held tight to myself, so I wouldn't fly away. I climbed to keep up. To find what we would find.

Our breathing came in gasps. Beside us, the earth fell away into darkness. Into the huge emptiness of the canyon crowded with spirits.

Spirits of the Blue Sky People. Of people poisoned by snakebites. Of people snatched by keeper holes. Of people drowned in the river.

The spirits of the dead.

Up and up we climbed, following the flickering flames. They licked the night, creating a small halo of light in the overwhelming darkness.

Breathing heavily, Willie stopped at a twisty, stunted tree. Its roots were clawing a big boulder on the edge of the sheer drop.

"This is where I turned back earlier," he said.

But now there was no turning back.

We took swigs from Roger's canteen, then marched on, up and up, following Willie's torch on the narrow path. Far below, the river rushed like a loud wind through a forest. The forest of the night.

Tyger, tyger, burning bright, in the forests of the night . . . I chanted insanely to myself. It was a poem by William Blake I had to memorize in Mrs. Gruber's class a month ago.

A million years ago.

"What are you muttering?" Lisa tugged on my shoulder.

"Nothing." I looked at my flashlight. It was half-dead, so I turned it off.

We climbed. It was cold, but I was sweating. Loose rocks tumbled down. I waited to hear a splash or a thunk into sand. Nothing. Just the sound of our feet, our breathing, the wind like a river or the river like the wind.

Suddenly, Willie tripped over something and sprawled across the path. I bumped into Lisa from behind and we both fell over. My flashlight bounced a few times, then flew over the cliff.

Roger stepped around us and knelt down. In the dusty blaze of the fallen torch, I could make out what Willie had tripped over.

A body! I thought I could make out a beard.

It was Dad! It had to be! It was my dad!

I couldn't breathe. If I could breathe I would have yelled, *DAD! Are you alive?*

Willie climbed to his knees, picked up the torch

with one hand, and set his other hand, on my dad's chest. A groan seemed to rise from deep inside him. Or was that me?

"Aaron?" A croak.

Dad was alive. *Alive!* I could breathe again.

"Aaron?" he moaned again.

"I'm here, Dad!" I scuttled beside him.

He coughed and croaked, "Water," just like a cartoon of a man dying in the desert.

But this was no cartoon. This was real life.

Roger tipped some water between Dad's lips. He gagged and most of it dribbled out. It mingled with the dried blood staining the side of his face. A bandanna was tied around the top of his head. It was blood-soaked too.

"Are you hurt, Dad?" I asked stupidly. Of course he was hurt. He was bleeding. He looked half-dead.

Suddenly, he looked dead. His head had lolled over. His eyes were half-open.

Roger gripped Dad's arm. "You still with us, buddy?"

Willie knelt down and put his ear to Dad's mouth. I held my breath.

"I can't hear anything . . . " Willie said.

I started to panic all over again.

"But I think I can feel some breath," Willie added.

He pressed two fingers to Dad's throat.

"Yep. There's a pulse. Not strong, but it's there." He turned toward us. "We've got to get him down from here. Quick. We've got to get help."

"We could be days from help, Willie," Roger said. Then he glanced at me. "But he'll live, Aaron. Your dad's tough. Tougher than he looks."

"Dad!" I felt like crying, but I didn't. My mind was racing. If I could just think fast enough, I could think of something that would save my dad.

"Cassidy!" Lisa said, out of the blue. "Where's Cassidy?"

Willie stared at her, his mouth grim. His eyes reflected the torchlight still flickering in his left hand.

"He's got to be nearby," Roger said. "He must have been carrying him."

That made sense. There was only one set of prints on the beach. And Dad was in no condition to walk. Why would Cassidy have gone on without my dad?

I didn't say it, but everyone must have been thinking it:

unless Cassidy fell over the side. Instinctively, I looked down over the cliff edge. We all did.

"*CASSIDY!*" Willie yelled.

We all joined in. "*CAASSIIIIIDDDDYYY!*"

Cassidy's name came echoing back, diminishing each time, like he was drifting further and further away.

"We've got to look for him," said Willie, waving his dying torch around, as if he could light up every corner of the universe with it.

"But what about my dad?" I yelled. "You said we had to get him help. That he could die here if we didn't."

As soon as those words left my mouth, I felt bad. If Cassidy was out there somewhere, alone in the dark, he needed our help too. We couldn't just leave him.

But what about my dad? Could we somehow help them both?

Willie just stared at me. He bit his lip and rubbed his grizzled face.

Roger closed his eyes and pinched the bridge of his nose.

Lisa looked down. But not at my dad.

My dad wasn't going anywhere.

And for the moment, neither were we.

Not without Cassidy.

"We'll have to split up," Roger said, after a long silence. "Me, Aaron, and Lisa will carry him down." He nodded toward my dad. "And Willie, you go find your son. We'll take one raft and—"

"We don't divide up, pard," Willie cut in. "We stick together. Just let me think!"

I knelt back down beside my dad. His eyes were closed now. I put my hand on his chest and I could feel it rise and fall. Barely. Barely.

"Just wait here," Willie said at last. "Just for a few minutes. This torch is dying. I need to make a new one. And I need to find Cassidy. My gut tells me he's not far. He's near and I've got to find him. I *will* find him."

But there's no time, I wanted to say. But I didn't. I loved my dad and Willie loved his son. You don't leave one for the other.

But what do you do?

It was what my dad would call a dilemma.

I felt like I had to grow up real fast. Like right now. And make a difference about my dad's fate. All our fates.

Even Cassidy's.

But how?

CHAPTER FIFTEEN

OVER THE EDGE

H ere," Willie said, handing me the dying torch. He pulled out his knife and slashed through another thick branch on a creosote bush. He lit it with a few flicks of his lighter and marched off.

Our eyes followed the glow of his torch, but soon it vanished into darkness. We could still hear him, but his footfalls dwindled, then disappeared.

Except for the sound of the river, the night was as silent as a dead man's heart.

Which reminded me. We hadn't done any first aid on Dad! It might not save him, but it should give him a better chance.

"Roger!" I said. "Your first aid kit! Anything in there that might help Dad?"

Roger seemed to snap out of a fog. I guess we were all pretty wasted. "Good thinking, mate! Let's take a look." He opened the first aid kit and I held the torch close while he fished around inside.

Then, with incredible speed, he had Dad's bandanna pulled off and his cut swabbed. It was an awful gash across his forehead, like a second mouth up there. Roger doused it in antiseptic and wrapped a bandage around his head.

"Got to make it tight," Roger said. "Helps staunch the blood."

Dad was out cold. Good thing, too, because he couldn't feel the pain, and we didn't have to hold his head to keep him from moving it. It's not an easy thing to see your dad unconscious and battered, with a bandage around his head.

Lisa scooted over and leaned her back against mine. We leaned against each other. We held each other up.

Roger paced back and forth, up and down the trail. He squatted and peered down over the edge into the darkness below.

"Aaron," he said. "Hand me that torch. Okay, mate?"

I gave it to him and he held what was left of it out before him, slowly sweeping it back and forth. "I think if he fell," Roger said, "he probably fell right here, where your dad fell when he dropped him."

If Cassidy fell, I thought, *he's long gone.* The drop-off just goes and goes. Clear down to the river. Without a brighter light, we couldn't see very far. But I lay flat anyway, with my head over the edge, and peered down. I willed my eyes to see in the dark. Willed them to gather all the invisible beams of starlight into one powerful beam and show me what I was looking for.

But I couldn't see him.

I sat back up and soon Lisa and I were leaning together again, keeping each other warm. I rubbed her arms and she rubbed mine. Roger disappeared up the trail. He couldn't sit still.

Time ticked by.

I heard a rustling sound in the scrub and then nothing. Maybe a deer.

My dad was wheezing softly now. Lisa and I slid down on either side of him and tried to keep him warm. We pressed against his sides and flung our arms over him. It felt weird hugging my dad like that, but the ground was so cold and we couldn't think of anything else to do. Time flowed by like the river below.

Suddenly, we heard a shout. I think it was Roger. It was

coming from higher up the trail. I couldn't make out what he was saying, but whatever it was, I couldn't just leave my dad here.

As if hearing my thoughts, Lisa said, "You go, Aaron. I'll stay with your dad. They might need your help carrying Cassidy. If they found him I mean."

"Are you sure? What if he wakes up and asks for me?"

"Go! You won't be gone more than a couple minutes. And you're wasting time. I got your dad covered. He's in good hands here. Trust me."

I did trust her.

I climbed to my feet and said, "Okay. Thanks, Lisa. But yell if he—"

"Go!" she said, with more urgency.

It was slow going in the dark, but my eyes had gotten used to it. Plus there was a hint of moon tipping the ridge and millions of stars sharing their brightness. I came upon them sooner than I expected, maybe four hundred yards up the trail. Roger and Willie were hunched over in the torch-light. Willie had wedged the flaming creosote between two rocks.

At their feet, the flickering light played over Cassidy's face. It was chalk white, like a wax mask.

"Is he . . ."

"He's alive," Roger said. "Hurt bad, but he'll live."

I knelt down beside them in the dirt path. Cassidy was unconscious, like my dad. Willie lifted the torch and in its wavering light I could see a jagged bone, sharp and white, poking out near the collar of his blood-stained shirt. I gagged, but managed not to lose my lunch.

But seeing Cassidy here, alive but badly hurt, threw my emotions into turmoil. I'd been holding so much anger toward him, always believing the worst. That he'd hurt my dad. Abandoned him. Maybe even killed him.

But now it didn't look like that could possibly be the true story of what happened. Someone had tied that bandana around my dad's head. Someone had carried him up this trail. And it made me wonder: maybe I'm the troubled one, not Cassidy.

"Thanks for coming, Aaron," Roger said. "We need your help to carry him. He's in pretty bad shape and if we're not careful we could make it worse."

Willie handed me the torch. It had burned down to a stub, but it was brighter than nothing. "He broke his collarbone. I think he fell under your dad's weight and snapped it. We're gonna try and cradle him, then stand him upright. You hold the torch with one hand, and hold his head up level with the other hand. Got it?"

"Got it."

"Okay," said Willie. "On three. One. Two. Three!" They lifted Cassidy upright and I held his head with one hand and the torch with the other. It was awkward. A head is way heavier than you'd imagine. I had to walk with my elbow jammed into my ribs to support the weight.

I felt like I was serving his head on a platter. An hour ago I would have been happy with the image, but now all that had changed.

With me in front, we slowly made our way back down the three or four switchbacks to where Lisa was waiting with my dad.

Dad. He hadn't moved, but his chest was rising and falling, so he was still alive.

"Oh my God!" Lisa cried. "You found him!" She jumped up, overjoyed. A thought popped into my head—would she have been that excited if it had been me—which I banished as quickly as I could. What is wrong with me?

"Okay now," Willie said, "we're going to lower him to the ground. Careful now. Careful."

Cassidy lay on his back, silent and still. Just like Dad.

Then his head rolled back and forth.

"Look!" Lisa yelped. "He's waking up!" She sat down beside him and put a hand on his forehead.

Cassidy started moaning and mumbling. His eyelids fluttered. Willie knelt beside him and spilled some water into his open mouth. Then he probed Cassidy's neck with his fingers.

"Aaagh!" Cassidy's eyes shot open. "Dude! Feels like. There's a spear stuck in me!" As he stutter-talked he reached up and touched the sharp protruding bone.

Lisa turned away and whispered to me, "Please tell me I didn't just see that." I guess in the dark, she hadn't seen the white bone till now.

Willie took Cassidy's hand and rubbed it. "We're gonna fix you up, son. Don't worry. Just lie still now. Tough it out."

Then he said to the rest of us, "We need to keep him warm. Your dad, too. They're both in shock. Anybody have any ideas?" He looked at each of us. Nobody was wearing any extra clothing. Actually, I had on a thin hoody but no way would it fit Cassidy or my dad.

"We've got to get them down from here, back to our camp," Roger said. "What do you think? Can they both be moved?"

"Got to," Willie said. He turned to me. "Your dad

probably has a nasty concussion to go with that cut. And he's lost a lot of blood. They're both suffering from exposure."

Now Willie turned to Cassidy and started rubbing his arms to bring back the circulation and warm him up. Cassidy tried to lift his head again, his eyes wild, and let out another groan.

"Whoa, hold it there, son," Willie said. "We're going to get you out of here. Soon. I promise. But first we've got to stabilize that collarbone a little. Roger? Hand me the first aid kit, will ya?"

With Roger's help, he wrapped a bandage in a figure eight, firmly crisscrossing Cassidy's shoulders and upper back.

"There, now try not to move anything. Play mummy. Can you do that, son?"

Cassidy started to nod, but stopped himself. It looked like he almost grinned.

Or was it a grimace? Hard to tell in the dying torchlight.

"How are we going to get them down?" I asked. I thought of fashioning one of those contraptions the Indians made with branches and blankets, like a stretcher you drag along the ground. . . . *A travois!*

I was about to say it aloud when Willie answered my question.

"Same way Cassidy got your dad up here," Willie said. "We'll carry 'em."

Then it really finally hit me—the truth of it. Cassidy

had carried my dad all the way up these cliffs. Like a mule! And me suspecting he'd killed him when I saw the lone set of prints on the beach.

But why had Cassidy carried my dad in the first place? Where was he going? Why didn't he just wait for us on the beach? And why did he leave Dad here on the path and go ahead, solo?

Even when I thought about it, it didn't make any sense.

But now was time to do, not think.

"Let's get your dad up first, pard," said Willie. He knelt and gently scooped his hands under my dad's shoulders. "Give me a hand."

Roger helped me hoist Dad onto Willie's broad shoulders, and Willie slowly stood up like a weightlifter. Dad's body drooped toward earth, like the earth was calling it back. Water, or blood, dripped to the ground.

Roger tried to scoop Cassidy up the same way, but Cassidy swatted him away. Lisa and I helped get him to his feet where he swayed like a drunk as Roger got under one arm and I got under the other. Lisa lifted the sputtering torch and walked ahead of us, lighting the way.

Cassidy strained and twisted, trying to pull away. He must be hallucinating or something.

"Lemme go!" he croaked.

Suddenly he wrenched free of us with a strength we didn't know he had. He took two steps, staggered . . .

. . . and toppled over the edge!

CHAPTER SIXTEEN

THE SPIRIT TRAIL

Lisa screamed. We both reacted instantly, lunging toward Cassidy, and we both almost flew over the cliff after him. I scrambled back, lay flat on my stomach, and peered down into the drop-off.

Lisa snatched the torch she'd dropped when she lunged. There was Cassidy. A branch of some scrubby pine tree growing out of a ledge had caught him by his flannel shirt. He hung there swinging over the void, just out of reach. The branch was bent like a fishing pole with a marlin on the hook. It looked like it could snap at any moment.

Willie said something but I wasn't listening. I scooted forward as much as I could and snatched a handful of Cassidy's shirt. He twisted and his shirt pulled up over his head. I heard a tearing sound. His shirt was ripping free.

I was going to lose him!

Willie must've lowered my dad back down to the ground, because suddenly he wrapped his arms around my legs and I was able to reach further down and grab Cassidy under his

arms. He screamed and I think he fainted. Then Roger flopped to his belly and I think he gripped Willie by his belt. Lisa must have grabbed his ankles, because the torchlight was gone.

Suddenly I could picture us: a human chain dangling over the cliff's edge.

"Lisa!" I called. "I need the light to see what I'm doing."

Lisa scurried to the edge, holding the dim torch over the side again. The torchlight trembled, then she held it firm. "Please don't drop him," she whispered.

I didn't say anything, I just held on. I wasn't going to let go. "We'll pull on three," I said. "One . . . two . . ."

On three, we heaved all together and yanked Cassidy back up over the edge.

We lay Cassidy flat on his back. Then we rolled onto our backs as well, panting from the effort. Cassidy and Dad were out cold. Lisa dropped the torch and I could hear it clattering down the cliff. She swore. Then she lay down beside us. We looked up at the stars. The Milky Way crossed the sky, thick as milk. I remembered Dad telling me once that some Native Americans called it the Spirit Trail—the trail the spirits took to the afterlife.

The river rushed through the night, like the sound of a storm coming. After a while, my blood finally slowed to a steady flow. I wondered how we'd all make it home.

While we were catching our breath, Cassidy woke up swearing. He tried to sit up and Willie caught hold of him and said, "Just lay still, son." But he couldn't lay still. He twisted and strained and swore.

Roger crawled away and came back with the first aid kit. He rummaged around in it, opened a jar, and tried to feed ibuprofen pills into Cassidy's mouth. To kill the pain. But Cassidy bit him and spit the pills out. Growled like a mad dog.

"Take it easy, mate," Roger said.

"Morphine?" Cassidy said. At least that's what I think he said. It was just a drunken jumble.

"No," Roger said. "But this will help. It's all we've got for painkillers." He got three or four pills pushed between Cassidy's lips and poured some water to wash them down. Cassidy twisted his head back and forth and spluttered, but I think some of the ibuprofen must've dissolved down between his teeth.

"We can't stay here all night," Willie said, climbing to his feet. "Cassidy might jump off that cliff again." He flapped dust off his knees and stretched. I could hear his spine crack. "We need to get them both down to warmth or they could die of exposure. Then we've got to get them down the river for help."

It seemed like an impossible task, but we had to make the impossible possible. What choice did we have? None.

I looked at Dad. He didn't say anything. He was still out cold.

Willie made another creosote torch and handed it to Lisa. He checked Dad's pulse and even pulled his lids back and looked at his eyes.

"Let's get this show on the road," he said.

We wrestled Cassidy to his feet as gently as possible, propping him between me and Roger. But this time we kept a strong grip on him, ready for anything. Cassidy was shivering and delirious, so he didn't put up a fight. Or maybe he'd learned his lesson.

Willie crouched down, and with help from Lisa, managed to sling Dad over his shoulders. "Let's vamoose," he said.

Lisa held up the torch and led the way. Willie trudged

behind her. Behind him and my dad, Roger and I half-walked and half-dragged Cassidy between us. He went in and out of consciousness, muttering, swearing, then growing silent again.

We inched along the winding path, in the flickering shadows of the torch and the slim light of a fingernail moon, afraid of slipping off the edge of the world.

"Goo c-catch, dude," Cassidy blurted out of the blue. He sounded drunk.

Was he talking to me?

"Almost went bye-bye." He started giggling . . . or crying, I couldn't tell which.

We stopped to rest, but not for long. Willie wanted to keep going. Cassidy was slick as a fish with cold sweat, and never stopped his mumbling. Dad was still unconscious and his bandage was soaked through with blood. Willie unwound it and asked Roger if there was another one in the first aid kit.

"Just one left, mate," Roger said. "No more after this." Then he took his bandanna off, doused it with water, and dabbed the blood from Dad's cut. He then tipped some antiseptic onto the last bandage and wrapped it tightly around Dad's head.

"Thanks, pard," said Willie, "you're a pro." Then, grunting like a bear, he heaved my dad to his shoulders again—without waiting for help from anybody—and started off back down the narrow path. Lisa leapt up and ran to squeeze ahead of them with the torch.

Roger and I got Cassidy wedged between us and followed. We stumbled along and Roger started to sing quietly in a croaky voice. It sounded a bit like a sea shanty. In that moment, I was filled with a strange feeling for Roger, Willie, Lisa, Dad—even for Cassidy. I guess you'd call it tenderness. I was feeling tenderness for everybody. And suddenly I felt like crying.

But I didn't. The tears just dammed there, clogging my brain.

We wound down and down. The path hadn't seemed nearly this long on the way up. Of course we weren't carrying any bodies then. Lisa's torch slowly burned out, but it didn't matter. We could see by the sliver of moon.

The Spirit Trail was hidden now beyond the ridge, but I knew it was still there. I hoped Dad wouldn't be walking along it before sunrise. We had to get help, but how?

I heard the hoot of a desert owl. It rippled through my blood and made me shiver. I couldn't wait for the darkness to end.

CHAPTER SEVENTEEN

RUNAWAY RAFT!

The sun was just beginning to light the sky to a pale gray by the time we made it back to camp. I thought I'd sigh with relief but I felt like I didn't have enough energy to even do that.

Roger and I laid Cassidy out next to Dad on a sleeping bag by the fire pit, where a few embers still glowed beneath gray ash. Then we covered them both with another open sleeping bag and added some wood to the coals. We had to get them warmed up fast.

I gazed down at Dad. Ugly purple bruises were starting to appear beneath his eyes. "That's a bad sign," Roger said. "Concussion's worse than I thought." The new—and last— bandage around Dad's head was already bloody. It made him look like a wounded soldier.

I walked to the river and slapped some freezing water on my face. Then Lisa and I gathered driftwood from up and down the bank. We brought back a pile and took turns chopping. Then we coaxed the almost dead fire back to life, while Roger and Willie attended to Dad and Cassidy.

I was completely exhausted—we all were—but there was no time to sleep. I was also famished. I hadn't eaten dinner last night and now hunger was stalking me like a wolf. I thought regretfully about the soup Lisa had offered to spoon-feed me, now spilled into the sand beside my tent.

Willie filled the kettle and snuggled it right on some coals as the morning light slowly seeped back into the world.

How were we all going to get out of this canyon alive?

While the kettle heated, we made plans. Roger unfolded a map and spread it flat across a boulder. Here, where we were now, the canyon walls fell straight down to the river with almost no beaches or flat areas. But, according to the map, about twenty miles downriver the canyon opened wide.

"Wide enough for a bush plane to land," Willie said.

"Now you're talkin', mate," Roger said.

A bush plane. I'd seen one, early in the trip, soaring high above the cliffs. The plan was to make the whole twenty miles downriver today to where, maybe, we could signal a bush plane to land.

It sounded like a good plan. Daunting, but good.

We wolfed down some gorp and coffee, pumped air into the rafts so they wouldn't ride sluggishly in the water, then broke camp in record time. Like I said, we were all exhausted—running on caffeine and adrenaline—yet we were on the river in under an hour.

Lisa went with Willie and Cassidy in the kitchen boat. I went with Roger and my dad, who was still out cold, stretched out in the bottom, wrapped in a tarp for warmth. I was starting to get scared. I mean, really scared. What if he slipped into a coma? What if he never woke up? What if we wrapped the boat or flipped over and his body got sucked down into a keeper hole.

What if.

Before we left the beach, we pulled Dad's raft up and tied it to a stump—we'd have to retrieve it later somehow. No way could Lisa or I have handled his boat. Not through what was coming. According to Roger: "The worst rapids of the river!"

Just what we needed.

What we really needed was to signal a plane and get my dad and Cassidy to a hospital "pronto," as Willie liked to say. But for the next twenty miles, all we could do was try to keep them as dry and comfortable as possible.

Cassidy was conscious again. We could hear him laughing and yelling in the kitchen boat. Laughing? What could he be laughing about? He sounded like a crazy loon.

The river was getting faster. It was great to be on it again, and for a moment I forgot about the terror of yesterday and last night.

But just for a moment.

Soon we hit Cascade, the first big rapid of the day.

"*Yee-haw! Ride 'em c-c-cow-ahh-baloney!*" Cassidy howled up ahead. Seemed like pain just made him giddy, I guess. He had one arm waving in the air, like a cowboy riding a rodeo bull. A cowboy on crack, that is. I can't imagine how that felt with a broken collarbone!

Roger was rowing, and I was on the back of the boat, trying to enjoy the ride like Cassidy. There were five drops in Cascade, one after another, and we were rollicking down like on a roller coaster when I heard something. *A plane!*

That's when I made a big mistake: I looked up.

Whoops! We hit a wave or a boulder and I bounced off the back of the raft, right into the white water!

Not again! I thought as I was churned inside nature's washing machine.

But this time I knew what to do.

Just as I started to gulp water, I popped to the surface and thrust my feet forward so I wouldn't smash my head on a rock. I didn't panic. I worked to keep my head above the waves, and before long it almost felt like I was bodysurfing in the ocean back home—but *on my back!*

Roger's raft was only about ten feet in front of me, but I couldn't swim toward it and still keep my feet in front of me. And Roger was too busy steering it to help me. I had to just float it out until we got to calmer waters.

Adrenaline pumped through me as I raced downriver on my back, bouncing off boulders like a pinball. I didn't always like wearing a life jacket, but I sure was glad I had it on now. Without it I'd be a goner.

Up ahead I could see a large boulder and what looked a lot like a keeper hole below it! I was even closer to the boat now, so with the last of my strength, I made a mad dash for it. It was now or never. Roger couldn't drop the oars to grab me, so I grabbed ahold of the frame, made one last wild kick with my legs, and thrust myself up and over the side of the raft.

I was back in! Wet and lying on the bottom of the raft, but back in. And I had done it all by myself!

Just as I was about to congratulate myself some more, I threw up. River water gushed out so hard it felt like I was heaving up the whole river.

I was shaking with cold and the electric rush of excitement.

"You shipshape, mate?" asked Roger.

I sat up, nodding. Roger dropped one oar and slapped my back, then grabbed back ahold before we could spin out of control.

I rinsed my mouth, and soon I felt pretty good again. Good about myself. Good about having some control over my own survival.

Then I looked down on Dad, who was still unconscious, and suddenly I was shivering again.

The water was calmer now, so I looked again to the sky, but there was no sign of the plane I'd heard. Gone.

We were in a swift flat stretch between tall gray cliffs, but already I could hear the roar of what was to come. And it wasn't a plane.

Roger rowed us into an eddy so we could scout Three Fords Rapid, the biggest rapid of our trip.

"In high water like this, Three Fords can be a Class 5 rapid," Roger warned. "There are lots of big boulders with deep holes behind them. And if you mess up, it's a half-mile swim out. A nasty swim."

There wasn't room for Willie's boat in our small eddy, so he pulled into an even smaller eddy upriver from us. Lisa waved. I waved back. Willie hopped out into waist-deep water and started hauling his raft into shore with the bowline.

"Whoa!" he yelled as the tail end of his raft got sucked back into the current. The whole boat began to swing downriver, spinning out of the eddy, and even Willie couldn't hold it.

"Lisa!" he shouted. *"Row!"*

Lisa jumped to the oars and dug a blade in, just as the line tore from Willie's grip.

With a sound like a gunshot, Lisa's oar snapped between two boulders, and the river took the kitchen raft—with Lisa and Cassidy— away.

"Runaway raft!" Willie bellowed.

Lisa tried to row with her one oar, but the raft just spun in spirals. Willie scrambled over the rocky shoreline and jumped into our raft, just as Roger pulled out into the current. He was trying to catch them before they hit the rapids.

But the runaway raft whipped right past us, a blur of blue rubber and black hair and flannel arms. They were out of reach and heading into the rapids with just one oar.

Into the worst rapids on the river.

We were already fifty yards behind them. Roger was rowing like a madman and I was kneeling in the bow, ready with the rescue line, Willie crouched beside me ready to jump. Lisa's raft—with Cassidy helpless within it—was plowing toward the first huge drop.

I clenched the rescue line. *I can do this,* I said to myself. *I can do this.*

CHAPTER EIGHTEEN

ROCK GARDEN

aron!" Roger shouted. "Get the spare oar!" It was lashed to the side of the raft. I dropped the rescue line, stepped over my unconscious dad, and began to loosen the straps holding it. But I couldn't get it free—it was snagged.

Lisa! I thought. *I have to do this right now!*

I forced my fingers to work harder and finally got the straps off it. I passed it forward to Willie, who held it over his shoulder like a spear.

Ahead of us, Lisa's raft was about to be funneled down the drop between two huge boulders when it got held up on one of them, thirty yards away.

Twenty, ten, five . . . Lisa's raft began to swing around the rock. She fought with her one oar, but the river was too strong. Just as she was about to be sucked down the rock-strewn current—what Willie had called a "rock garden"—he leapt like a wild man, holding the oar like a spear, and landed in the back of Lisa's boat. They plunged over the drop and away from view.

But there was the oar, snagged between two boulders! Willie must have dropped it. Maybe I could reach it. I flopped on my belly and leaned out so far over the water that I was sure I'd topple in again, but I was just able to snatch the oar at the last second and pull it in.

There was no time to lose.

We came crashing down behind them, maybe thirty feet back, right into a rock garden. Ahead of us, they were spinning wildly out of control, banging into rocks every few feet. Willie propped himself in the back of his raft, but he was clutching his shoulder like he was in serious pain.

How am I going to get this oar to them? I thought. *And how is Willie going to catch it if he hurt his shoulder?*

"THROW IT!" Willie shouted.

What if I miss? What if I don't miss but hit Willie or Cassidy or Lisa with the oar?

Enough with the what ifs.

I took a deep breath, cocked the oar back, and heaved it forward with all I had. It flew straight through the air just like a javelin . . .

. . . and landed right on target!

Willie snatched it out of the air with his giant hands and hooked it into the oarlock, then clutched his shoulder again! He really was hurt.

Lisa yelled something at him and he moved aside so she could scoot back into the seat. Within seconds she was rowing like crazy.

Then they disappeared down the next drop.

We were about twenty feet behind them and the nose of our raft tipped down. It was like crashing down a waterfall.

WHOOOOSH!

"Hold on!" Roger yelled.

"High side! High side!" Roger hollered, and I climbed up. With me clinging to the high side, the boat slid back down. Then I hopped back to the bow to watch for obstacles. Roger powered us through haystack waves eight feet tall, all the while dodging holes and bouncing off boulders.

Right then I dubbed him Roger Dodger. From now on he

was Roger Dodger as well as Roger the Rogue.

And there was the kitchen boat on course, dancing down the river ahead of us—Lisa rowing like a wild woman, and Willie in the bow calling the shots.

They whipped around boulders and holes, disappearing a few times, reemerging and disappearing again.

Like Willie, I was in the bow, calling the shots. "Stay river right!"

Finally, after the wildest ride of the trip, we all sailed out of danger and into calm waters again. I let out a whoop. Willie and Lisa whooped back.

When we caught up to them, I stood up, soaking wet, and yelled, "Lisa! Are you alive?"

"I am if you are!"

"Good job rowing!" I yelled.

"Good job throwing!" she yelled back.

Lisa raised both hands, making victory signs, and gave me a grin as big as Texas. Then grabbed the oars again.

And yes, I felt more alive than I had ever felt in my life.

Maybe Cassidy had been right, I thought, *about the power of danger.*

I think what he was talking about was overcoming it. And yes, overcoming it does fill you with, if not power, at least confidence.

Cassidy. He was dead to the world again. He had come too close to that edge he'd talked about. I might be feeling super alive now, but I bet Cassidy was feeling closer to dead.

If he was feeling anything at all.

What about Dad? I'd almost forgotten about him during the time it took us to get through the rapids. Like Cassidy, he was still out cold. He was also soaking wet and looked like he'd been tossed around like a rag doll. But he was all in one piece. Thank God.

I started to shiver again. I don't know if it was from my wet clothes in the rising wind, or from seeing Dad there, still unconscious.

I spelled Roger at the oars.

"Thanks, mate," he said, the pirate back in his voice and

the twinkle back in his eye. "You saved the day, Aaron."

There was no time for the compliment to sink in, to celebrate. We had to get to where a plane could land before dark. And we still had a long way to go.

Ahead of us, after a brief effort by Willie, Lisa was at the oars again. She was pulling in strong, smooth strokes. I tried to keep up with her, but it took all my strength. We hit one rapid after another, Roger barking out orders and warnings about boulders and holes. Spray climbed the steep rock walls and waves broke over us.

Vultures circled high overhead, in the endless blue of the sky. I hoped they weren't waiting for us.

We were rolling along at a good clip when we smelled rotten eggs.

"Must be Coal Creek Rapids," Roger said. "Sulfur hot springs give it that lovely fragrance." He stood up and made the eddy-out signal, and Lisa pulled into shore.

"Better scout this one out, mate," Roger said.

Willie rubbed his shoulder, then tied their raft with extra care this time. Guess he didn't want any more runaways.

"How's your shoulder, mate?" Roger asked.

"Don't worry about me, pard. Let's get the real invalids to safety."

Then we scrambled up a rock path to where we had a good view of the rapids.

"Howdy, slowpoke," Lisa teased. "But that really was some throw back there, Aaron. You were pretty awesome."

This time the compliment took my breath away. I couldn't even answer her.

Fortunately, Willie butted in, slapping me on the back with his good arm, "Yep, Aaron's a real hero all right." A blush heated my face. Then he added that Lisa was a hero too, and went immediately back to business.

"Another rock garden ahead," he said, pointing to the river. We looked down at the rapids below, a roaring maze of holes and boulders and waves.

I studied it carefully. All of a sudden, it made sense—boulders and currents fell into place and I could see a path snaking downriver. It was like reading words on a page—for the first time.

"I think I see a way through it," I said, and told them the route I saw.

"Not bad, mate," Roger said, "Not bad. You're learning to read the river like us old river rats!"

I beamed. Lisa elbowed me. "You old river rat." Then she pinched her nose and said, "And you smell like one, too."

It amazed me that we could joke around like this when so much was riding on the next several hours. Our way of letting off steam, I guess.

This time Lisa got in our boat. Willie wanted to lighten up the heavier kitchen boat. He was afraid of getting stuck on a boulder. And he swore that he was "shipshape" when Roger asked him about his shoulder.

Cassidy had come to again. He yelled something, but it

didn't make any sense. He was grinning weirdly, but his teeth were chattering and his eyes looked as red as hot coals. I noticed my anger toward him had melted away, like clouds on a summer day. All I felt for him now was sympathy. And gratitude—assuming he did save my dad.

I was still full of questions, but one look at Dad, who was still out cold and looking worse than ever, and I knew we had to act now and save our questions for later.

Willie and Cassidy went first. He eased out into the current, slid downstream, angling toward the cut bank, then shot into the rapids. We waited half a minute, then nosed into the current and followed.

I sat in the bow, shouting warnings. Lisa curled down in the bottom, trying to keep my dad from bouncing around too much. Roger spun the boat around, then we plunged into the chaos and violence of the rapids.

We were on a mission. A mission to save Dad and Cassidy. A mission to save us all. And no rapids were going to stop us.

We came around a bend and there was Willie. His boat, with Cassidy and all the kitchen gear, was still too heavy and was stuck atop a submerged boulder, the river raging around it. Willie was rowing with all his strength, but the raft wouldn't budge.

"Throw the rescue line, Aaron!" Roger commanded, as we bounced toward them.

As we came even with their boat, I was ready. With my knees and toes wedged securely against the tubes, I flung the line out with all my might. The nylon rope uncoiled as it sailed through the air toward Willie.

But we were moving super fast, and Willie clutched his shoulder just as I threw it, so the line flew just over his head as we shot by. I tried pulling it back in for another attempt, but it was too late.

Willie yelled something—or was it Cassidy? Whoever it was, the roar of the river drowned them out. They vanished from sight behind us as we were swept around the bend and down through what Coal Creek Rapids had to offer.

There was no turning back. Willie and Cassidy were on their own.

CHAPTER NINETEEN

THE THUNDER HOLE

aron!" Roger shouted. "We have to find a place to eddy out!" I knelt in the bow. A sheer wall on one side, giant chunks of rock on the other. We rounded another bend and there, behind a tall boulder to the right, was a small eddy of smooth water. I pointed and Roger gave our raft a spin and pulled out of the rampaging current and into the tiny cove.

There was no beach, so I had to jump into thigh-high water and tie the bowline around a rock. Roger hopped out and immediately began scrambling over boulders, heading back upriver. Swallows were swooping and darting overhead, as a fine mist rose above the roar of the rapids. Lisa climbed after Roger like a mountain goat, and I followed behind her.

We quickly reached a spot where we couldn't go any further. We were at a cliff with a straight drop of seventy, eighty feet or more, right down into the boiling cauldron of the rapids. And no visible path across it. We pulled ourselves up on a ledge beside Roger and looked upriver.

There was Willie still hung up on the boulder! He was

maybe two hundred feet upriver and standing on his raft. No. He was jumping from one side to the other, right over Cassidy's body—rocking the boat! *Jump. Jump. Jump.* He jumped one last time and suddenly his raft wobbled . . . tottered . . . and slid off the boulder!

It whirled free and raced down the river, Willie back at the oars. We whooped and cheered as they flew by.

"Wild Man Willie does it again!" Roger howled. "Let's go, me lad and lassie!"

When we got back to our raft we had a big surprise: Dad was awake!

"Dad!" I cried, so relieved he wasn't in a coma.

But he didn't answer me. He didn't even look at me, just mumbled some nonsense. He was delirious. I thought I heard him say Cassidy's name. Was he replaying those last moments before his boat flipped?

How did their boat flip? I asked myself for the hundredth time. Had there been a fight over the oars? Maybe Dad wanted to help row against that wind but Cassidy was too macho to let him. Maybe Dad stood up and without his weight on the bow the boat flipped. Or did it flip after a fight? Maybe Cassidy swung his oar and Dad fell in, tipping the raft. Cassidy, feeling guilty, might have dived in after him. But then why did he leave him on the trail?

I was dying to ask Dad and Cassidy all these questions. When there was more time. And when they were coherent. But when would that be?

"Here, Dad, drink this." I tipped some water from my canteen onto his lips. His head rolled from side to side and the water spilled down his chin. I had to try again. I was afraid he'd die of dehydration. Dehydrated on a river, with water all around!

"Water, water, everywhere, but nary a drop to drink," I mumbled to myself.

Wasn't that from a poem or a song or something? I tried giving him water again. Finally some seeped in and Dad licked his lips. They were cracked and swollen. Parched dry as the desert itself. Within seconds, the water trickled out again. Dad gagged and coughed and I turned his head so the rest could spill out and not get into his lungs. There was nothing else I could do.

"When we join up with the kitchen boat," Roger said, "we'll look for a funnel. Might help. For now, it helps to at least keep his lips and tongue and mouth wet, or they'll get worse."

Roger unwrapped the bandage and rinsed the blood out in the river. He changed the dressing on Dad's gash and added some more antiseptic before rewinding the wet bandage around his head. Lisa tried to soothe him with a cool wet cloth and a soft hum.

It was hard to know when to cool him and when to warm him. He was still wrapped in a tarp but was pretty wet from the waves crashing in. Meanwhile, the sun blazed down. Still not a cloud in the sky.

"We're almost there, Dad," I said, not really knowing where "there" was or what would happen when we finally arrived. I wanted to reassure him, but there was no time to linger. We had to keep moving.

It was a race against the clock. And if the clock stopped ticking, so did Dad.

We caught up to Willie when he pulled over to scout Rattlesnake Rapid, which we could hear roaring downriver. Cassidy was propped up inside the raft. He was grimacing, blinking his eyes and mumbling.

"Hey, Cass," Lisa called out, "my dad told me one of the Wild Bunch got shot here."

Was it a trick of the light, or did Cassidy's eyes open at the sound of her voice?

"Yeah," Roger added, "a guy named Flat Nose Curry. He got a fatal dose of Western justice right around here."

Lisa and I followed Roger and Willie up the wall of the canyon to a rocky ledge and looked down at the next set of rapids.

"Rattlesnake," Willie said. "Another killer." There were at least a dozen boulders jutting out of the water. There were several deep holes among the haystack waves. I tried to read the river again, looking for the main current, looking for a path.

"There's the tongue," I said, pointing. "We enter it from the right, then slide to the left around that boulder there— the one that looks like a skull. . . ."

"Good eye, pard," Willie said.

But Roger said, "Yeah, good eye, mate, but I think we should shoot straight down the left side, and try to avoid that boulder all together."

"If we can," Willie said, "that would be the best."

I didn't agree. I thought the current would suck us around the boulder, but I held my tongue. They had way more experience than I did.

We scrambled down into our boats and Willie took off in the lead. After a minute, we slipped into the current behind them.

This time Lisa sat on the bow and I sat in back with Dad. We hit the rapids and slid into the tongue from the left. Suddenly, the current grabbed hold of us, gripped us in its coils, and whipped us to the right. We dropped and spun like a teacup, right around the boulder that looked like a skull.

Too close! The boat whiplashed with a jerk and I flew into Roger. Lisa screamed, but held on.

We slammed against the backside of the boulder and I could feel the front pulling toward a dark, swirling funnel.

"Keeper hole!" Roger yelled. I could barely hear him over the thundering water. This was more than just a keeper hole. It sounded like a thunder hole to me.

Our raft was trapped against the boulder by a back wave. If we slid off, we'd be snatched by the whirlpool and spun round and round. If we flipped or fell in, we'd be sucked down.

And never come back up.

"High side! High side!" I shouted.

Lisa and I leapt up and clung to the side that was riding up the boulder. I had to hang on to Dad at the same time, or he could topple in.

And if he toppled in, he'd be a goner for sure.

Willie was downriver, out of sight. We were stuck alone on the edge of doom.

The river started tumbling in, filling the raft faster than the raft could self-bail. The whirlpool was pulling us in, tugging us down like a pack of vicious water babies.

The thunder hole had us.

"Bail! Bail!" Roger shouted. Lisa unclamped the bail bucket and started scooping water out, as quickly as a dog digs sand. Roger let go of an oar to join me on the high side and help hold Dad. The oar blade caught in the edge of the whirlpool and the handle smacked into Roger's elbow. He yelped with pain and cupped his elbow.

Roger jumped beside me on the high side and clamped his good arm and both legs around my dad. With the extra weight, the raft started to slide down toward the lip of the hole.

"We've got to row out of here," I said, "or the hole will suck us in! I'll row! You stay high side and hold my dad!"

"There's no way you're strong enough, mate!"

"Lisa can help!" I countered, and jumped toward the seat.

"You got that right!" Lisa said. She had bailed enough. She jumped up to the oars and sat down, facing me. I swung my leg out and kicked off from the boulder just enough to wedge the high side oar in. Then Lisa grabbed hold of both oars, placing her hands next to mine.

"Go for it!" Roger yelled. "And follow your own route!"

Lisa and I had to coordinate. She would push when I pulled.

"Push!" I called, as I pulled with all my strength. And together we rowed so hard on the wooden oar that it actually started to bend.

"Pull!"

"Push!"

"Pull!"

Lisa and I were a team and I knew that together we could do this. We could save the day.

And my dad.

CHAPTER TWENTY

RACING FOR RESCUE

We pushed and pulled with our legs and arms and backs, straining every muscle in our bodies.

We were still sliding toward the hole when suddenly the edge of the whirlpool caught the nose of our raft, ripping us away from the boulder and spinning us around.

"We have to turn counterclockwise!" I yelled. We dug an oar in and helped the nose pivot in the whirlpool so that the tail of the raft swung back out, snagged by the main current. Then with all our might we rowed away from the whirlpool. It was a tug-of-war between the current and the keeper hole, with Lisa and me on the side of the current.

We won! The whirlpool spit us out and our raft spun free.

Lisa and I whooped. *"YAHOO!"*

"YEAH!" yelled Roger. We would've slapped high fives but we didn't dare let go of the oars. There was still more to this rapid. A lot more.

"Great work, mateys!" Roger was so happy he pumped

his fists in the air. Then his face crumpled in pain and he cradled his bruised elbow.

Now that we were back on course—my course—down the rapids, Roger was able to slide down next to Dad and rest. I guess he figured we didn't need his help anymore.

Lisa and I stayed at the oars, snaking down Rattlesnake Rapids. Before we had a chance to catch our breath, we were pinballing off boulders again in Nefertiti Rapids just below.

As much as I wanted to relax, there was no time for it. Dad was moaning again. He looked like a mummy wrapped in that tarp. We had to keep going. Keep up to speed.

Lisa and I rowed, our bodies going through the motions, numb with exhaustion.

Roger closed his eyes as he said, "Lemme know when you two need a break, mateys. I'm gonna rest my eyes for a bit, but this Captain's ready to row any time."

"We're good," I said. "Right, Lisa?"

"Totally." We both kicked ourselves into gear. It was like we'd gotten a second wind.

We ran one more set of rapids, which Roger kept mum through, and it was awesome. From the thunder hole to here, it was our first time running rapids with just the two of us, no adults barking orders. We breezed right through, and slapped high fives at the far end.

"That was awesome!" I said.

"I know, right?" Her smile was so big I thought her teeth would fall out.

She hopped over and sat up on the tube in the bow, facing me and said, "Let me know when you want me to spell you, Aaron."

I started to say, "I can spell Aaron. A, A . . ." but just then we rounded a bend and the canyon opened out like a fan. There were wide stretches of flat desert between the river and the high canyon walls.

Room for a plane.

"There's Willie!" I hollered. Lisa joined me again at the oars and we rowed for the shore for all we were worth.

Finally, after twenty miles through the hardest rapids of the river, we eddied out. Lisa and I jumped up and did a little dance in the bow.

"*YAHOOOOOOO!*"

"Keeper hole almost swallowed us," Roger said, hopping onto the beach.

"Wondered what took you so long, pard," Willie said. He didn't stop to chat, but walked down the beach collecting wood and brush in his arms. He already had a big pile gathered and burning up the beach. I could see Cassidy next to it in a sleeping bag. His face was ghost white.

"Got to get this fire smokin' before dark," Willie continued. "We need a plane—*now!*"

We carried Dad to the fire and wrapped him up in a sleeping bag next to Cassidy. The sun was sinking toward the western ridge and the far cliffs already glowed a blood red.

A chill crept into my bones even though the fire was big and hot. It was getting dark fast, but we hadn't heard a plane since early morning. What were the chances?

"We need more smoke!" Willie bellowed. "More firewood! Everybody. *Pronto!*" Lisa and I scrambled across the dry flats, scrounging up dead, fallen mesquite and creosote branches, and carrying them back to the fire.

I was exhausted, stumbling over roots and stones. I wanted to sleep. Or at least to sit and rest. And I was starving too. Nothing but gorp all day. But I could see Roger and Willie hustling around and I felt their urgency and forced myself to move faster. The faster I worked the more urgency I felt.

I knew that if we didn't signal a plane before dark and get Dad to a hospital, he'd have a hard time surviving another night. We hadn't been able to get any fluids into him all day. Roger said he was totally dehydrated. He was also wheezing and had lost a lot of blood.

More than ever, I was really, really scared. For Dad, it was do or die time.

Fear can freeze you or give you a jolt. In this case, it gave me a jolt. I moved faster than ever, spilling armfuls of wood next to the fire and racing back for more. Lisa was doing the same, and it wasn't even her dad that was in danger.

I think I loved her in that moment. No, not that way! Just, you know. I was just so grateful that she understood how I felt and wanted to help.

While Lisa and I scurried around like beavers, Willie built a roaring bonfire. Yellow flames stretched up into the sky, licking at the darkening air. Lisa and I tossed on bark and leaves, damp driftwood, and green branches we'd found beneath the cottonwoods. Smoke billowed up in giant puffs, hopefully big enough for a plane to see.

"That's the idea!" Willie yelled. "Keep it coming!"

"Now we're smokin'!" Cassidy said. He was awake! He was still propped against the stump and his eyes were wide open. "Who wants burgers and fries?" he said with a giggle.

I was staring at Cassidy, waiting to hear about his next hallucination when I heard something else: a drone. Like a lawn mower. It was getting louder and louder, closer and closer. I froze and scanned the sky. I felt as alert as a hungry dog staring at a juicy bone.

Finally, up over the ridge buzzed a little bush plane! It roared through the canyon, straight toward us. We dropped our loads of wood and raced out to the sand flats to watch it land. Willie was shouting and waving his arms over his head.

"Wait!" Willie hollered. "It has pontoons!"

It was some kind of seaplane! We all tore back through the brush and sand to the riverbank, anxious to see the plane come skidding along the river.

But it didn't! The plane kept going, dragging my heart right along with it.

Why didn't it land? Didn't the pilot see us?

It flew low over the river, right past where we were standing on the shore, waving our arms and jumping up and down. It went right past, upriver toward a dark bend in the canyon. It rounded the bend and kept going, out of sight.

I couldn't believe it.

"NO-O-O-O!" I shouted. "NO!"

CHAPTER TWENTY-ONE

TIME TO GO!

As the buzz of the engine got quieter and quieter, Willie's ranting got louder and louder. He was slinging a string of swearwords like firecrackers at that vanished plane. I was still jumping and yelling and waving with Lisa, like lost puppets on a string.

Roger stood speechless—uncharacteristically speechless—hands clamped to his hips, legs planted wide apart.

The sun sank beyond the ridge and my heart sank with it. Willie stopped cursing.

And then I heard it again. The drone of the plane! It was coming.

It was coming back!

Roger and Willie joined Lisa and me in our crazy jumping-jack dance. And slowly, slowly the little tin can with wings reappeared. It swooped over us, then skidded along the water not far away, trailing a rooster tail of spray.

We howled and cheered beneath the deafening sound of the engine, and I suddenly found Lisa pressed against me.

I hugged her back. We rocked back and forth and I didn't want to let go. Ever.

But the next thing I knew she was in Roger's arms, and Willie's arms, and then we were all doing a big group hug. Kind of embarrassing, but what can I say?

The plane taxied toward us and I could read BLM—Bureau of Land Management—printed on its side. It drifted to a stop and the door opened. The uniformed pilot, a big bear of a man with a bushy red beard, stepped out onto a pontoon and tossed us a line. Willie caught it and Roger and I helped him pull the plane in.

When it got close enough, the pilot jumped ashore, splashing in the last few inches of water. Willie tied the line off around a snarl of roots.

"What do we have here?" said the pilot in a hearty voice. "A bunch of river rats having a party?"

"The Wild Bunch," cracked Cassidy from over by the fire. You could see that he was hurting, but you could also see that he was coming around. He was coherent for the first time in a long time.

"We had an accident," Roger said. "The boy here has a broken collarbone and the man wrapped in the tarp probably has a concussion and then some. He hasn't been conscious all day. Can you give them a lift to the hospital in Green River?"

"Sure. But I only have room for the two injured ones. Good thing I saw the smoke," the pilot added. "I was about to call it a day. Sorry to scare you like that, but I wanted to turn around to get the wind behind me for the landing."

"We're just happy you came back," I said. That was the understatement of the year.

"The rest of us will row to the pullout at dawn," Roger said. "We should be able to break down the rafts, load up, and make it to Green River by noon, I'm guessing."

"Sounds about right," said the pilot.

"I've got some coffee ready," Willie told him. "Cup to go?"

"A pilot needs coffee like a plane needs fuel," the pilot said with a grin. He peered up at the sky. The light was seeping away toward the west and dark was painting the cliff walls. "Three minutes!" he said, concern deepening the creases of his weathered face. "Then we gotta go."

"Water," croaked a voice behind us. It was Dad! He was propped up on one elbow watching us. His bandage was bloodier than ever and his cheekbones looked like twin sunsets. But he was conscious!

Willie tossed me a canteen and I knelt and tipped water into his mouth. This time it slipped between his parched lips and stayed in. His Adam's apple jerked up and down like the trigger of a pistol. He looked bad, but he was alive and glugging water. I breathed a huge sigh of relief.

"This boy here," Dad rasped, nodding to Cassidy. "He . . . he . . ."

We were all dead silent as we waited for his next words.

"He saved my life," Dad said with a sigh, like he'd just

dropped a terrible load from his shoulders. He couldn't talk anymore and slumped back to the ground.

We all looked at Cassidy.

"What happened back there, son?" Willie said, squatting beside him as he poured some steaming coffee into a tin mug for the pilot.

"Dude. The wind. It flipped us." His voice sounded like sandpaper. "He busted his head open on an oarlock and fell into the river. We both did. He was drowning. I was able to grab him before the current did, and drag him to shore. He was out, man. Scalp leaking like a rusty faucet. The raft had snagged on a log and I was able to pull it in to shore too. Then I gave your dad some CPR."

The pilot blew on his coffee.

"So why did you carry him off the beach?" Roger asked. "Why didn't you wait for us?"

"Dude! I figured you guys would hole up all night to wait out the wind. So I decided we needed to get out of the canyon and try to signal a plane or this old man was gonna bite it, you know?"

"He could yet," said the pilot, suddenly jumping to his feet. "If I don't catch the last bit of light and get him to the medical clinic in Green River. Gotta get you there too, young man, by the look of things. Get you patched up."

The burly pilot blew on his coffee once more and slurped one loud sip. He dashed the rest of it into the sand and said, "Time to go!"

As I helped Cassidy to his feet and walked him toward the plane, I asked him the last question that had been plaguing me for so long: "When you fell and broke your collarbone, why did you leave my dad on the trail and go on ahead? I don't get it."

Cassidy laughed. "Why do you think? I had to crawl out from beneath him and then I just kept on crawling. I thought I could make it up to the plateau and flag a plane down. Like this one, here."

"In the dark?"

"It woulda been dawn, dummy."

I sat Cassidy down next to the plane, then helped the pilot unload and carry a rolled-up stretcher back to the fire for my dad. It was just starting to sink in, the awesomeness of what Cassidy had done, as I helped load my dad, as gently as possible, onto the stretcher.

Roger, Willie, Lisa, and I each grabbed a handle and lifted Dad up. As we neared the plane, Dad called out, "Wait!"

"Cassidy," he rasped. "Thanks, man." His bloodshot eyes welled with tears.

And for the first time on the trip, so did mine.

"You're okay, dude," Cassidy said, holding Dad's gaze for

a long second. Then we wrestled the stretcher into the back of the cockpit.

"Hang in there, Dad!" I said, squeezing his hand. "You'll be up and kicking in no time! We'll row out of here first thing in the morning and come straight to the hospital and see you."

For a moment—just a moment—it felt like I was the father and he the son.

Dad made a little wave of his hand, then his eyes closed. He seemed to be at peace, maybe already asleep.

Next, Lisa and I jumped down to help Cassidy into the plane. We each hooked an arm around him, being careful of his collarbone. Between us, we stumble-walked him to the plane, then helped him aboard. Once we got him onto the pontoon, I looked at him, as if seeing him for the first time.

"Thanks for saving my dad, Cassidy," I said. "I owe you one." It wasn't easy for me to say it.

"Anytime, dude," he said. "I owe you one, too. For snatching me off that branch before it snapped. I woulda bit it for sure. And Lisa," he turned to her, "next time I'm in a runaway raft, I hope you're there to save my butt again."

Cassidy grinned at us. A real smile, not a smirk or a sneer.

We stood stunned and speechless, maybe even a little embarrassed. Who knew Cassidy could ever be a nice, normal guy? Lisa broke the awkward moment by giving Cassidy a half-hug. I could see him wincing from the pain. Finally, Lisa pulled away and Cassidy gave me a nod.

"Later, dude," he said, ducking inside the crowded cockpit.

"Later, Cassidy."

I yelled good-bye to my dad and jumped into the shallows. I was filled to overflowing. With all of it. The trip, the emotions, everything.

And suddenly the tears that had been welling in my eyes overflowed, like a dam bursting.

I turned away so no one would see and wiped my cheeks. Then I turned back and watched Willie and Roger untie the line and push the plane out into the current.

We waved as the pilot fired up the engine, taxied out, and slowly gathered speed. Soon the plane roared down the river and lifted off.

It quickly shrunk to the size of a bird in the twilight, its wings as thin as the line between hope and despair.

CHAPTER TWENTY-TWO

OLYMPIC CHAMP

The night was bursting with stars and, despite our exhaustion, we sat around the fire eating and celebrating. And talked about Cassidy.

"Oh man," I said. "I can't get over what he did. What he was able to do. He was actually planning to carry my dad clear up to the Tavaputs Plateau, and wave down a plane." The thought was so huge and airy that it stopped me talking but kept me thinking. *Wow! He did all that and he didn't even like my dad. Maybe even hated him. What a guy.*

"Yeah, he must've stumbled on a root or something," Willie said. "Then in his delirium, he kept on going, trying to reach the top. That boy's got more guts than sense."

"But how's it possible for him to carry a grown man so far up that steep trail?" Lisa asked.

"He pumps iron," Willie said. "Bench-presses two hundred pounds."

Lisa elbowed me. "How much can you bench-press, Aaron? That's about twice as much as you weigh! Am I right?"

I made a fist and shook it at her. She made a fist back. Then she said, "You ever think of throwing the javelin, Aaron? The way you threw that oar, you might become an Olympic champ yet!" The whites of her teeth almost knocked me into the fire.

"Yarrr," said Roger with his pirate growl. "Ye make a fine scallywag in a pinch, me good man, Aaron!"

And so does Cassidy, I thought.

We all talked at once then, and went back to filling our faces. Wild Man Willie had made a feast with a ten-pound slab of New York steak and a dozen baked potatoes.

It was quite possibly the best meal I had ever eaten and probably ever will.

That night, as overtired as I was, I lay awake, alone, in our tent, listening to the river making its midnight utterances.

Being here now without Dad made me think about him, the trip, all of it. I thought about the eighty-four miles we had rafted down the Green River, the beauty of the canyon, the peace of the river. I also thought about the terror of some of those rapids and the terror of almost losing my dad. I felt, well, grateful about being able to marvel at it all. And about being able to balance the beauty and the terror. And I felt good about myself, for a change. I didn't freeze when Cassidy fell off the cliff. I followed my instinct and sprang. And I jumped to the oars when I was most needed. Like Roger had said, I was "a fine scallywag in a pinch." And who knew, maybe Lisa was right that I could be "an Olympic champ yet."

Lisa. For the first time, I felt like there was a girl out there who really liked me. Liked being with me, liked who I am. I could even talk to her! My tongue, at least for now, no longer got tied into impossible knots whenever we spoke. Maybe we could stay friends, even after the trip. Weirder things have happened, right?

The last thing I remember before falling asleep, like a stone sinking into a deep pool, was the sound of the river passing twenty feet from my head. And what Dad had said that first day, about how I'd learn to read the river like a pro.

Thanks, Dad. I had learned to read the river and I liked what I read.

And, now that I thought about it, I was even starting to like myself.

EPILOGUE

In the morning, we broke camp and rowed the last easy stretch to the take-out at Swasey's Rapid. There, we deflated the rafts, folded them, and carried all the gear to our waiting pickup truck and van. Chores finished, we drove the ten miles to the medical clinic in Green River to see Cassidy and my dad.

But when we got there, they were gone!

A nurse told us they'd been airlifted by helicopter to a hospital in Salt Lake City. We stood there in the reception room, stunned.

But then the nurse explained that they'd treated Cassidy and my dad for exposure and dehydration, stitched Dad's forehead, and gotten their conditions stabilized. But Dad, because of his concussion, needed to be checked for head trauma. Plus, Cassidy's broken collarbone was a compound fracture and he needed immediate surgery. So off they had gone, even further away from us. The nurse told us not to worry and helped us call the hospital in Salt Lake City.

The doctor there told us Dad had gotten an MRI and a CT scan and his brain was fine. Phew! I wanted to talk to him but he was asleep. The doctor said his condition was stable and they wanted to keep him under observation for one more night. If all went well—and the doctor assured me that it would—Dad would be released the next day at noon.

Willie talked to the doctor next. Apparently, the surgery on Cassidy's fracture had gone smoothly and there was nothing to worry about. They had screwed a steel plate into his shattered collarbone and it would take about two months to heal.

On the long drive to Salt Lake City, Lisa sat beside me in Roger's battered old pickup. Her arm pressed against mine as we bounced along the highway through Utah's high desert. I didn't lean away.

"So you want to do this again next year?" she asked. "We might go down the Owyhee or the Snake. We might even do a kayak trip next time."

"Do you want to?" I asked.

"If you do."

"Me too."

"What if Cassidy goes?" She smiled and looked deep inside me with those big dark eyes.

I thought about it for a moment.

"Sure," I said.

And I meant it.

DISCUSSION QUESTIONS

1. *Describe* Desolation Canyon's *younger characters: Aaron, Lisa, and Cassidy. How are they alike, and how are they different? Which of the three characters can you relate to the most? Why? Give examples from the book to support your answer.*

2. *How would you describe Cassidy's behavior toward Aaron? Have you or one of your friends ever been in a similar situation? What do you think about Aaron's responses to Cassidy? Do you think the adults should have intervened more? If so, how?*

3. *How would the story have been different if it had been written from Cassidy's or Lisa's point of view instead of Aaron's?*

4.   *What is the setting for this story? How does the setting help drive the plot? Can you think of another setting that would offer the same types of challenges?*

5.   *"Hey, pard. How ya doin'?" is an example of dialect. How does the author's use of dialect add to or take away from the story? Give examples from the book.*

6.   *The characters in this story survive many difficult challenges, both physical and emotional. Describe one obstacle a character overcomes in this story. Include details from the book about the problem and how it was solved.*

7.   *Like a white-water rafting trip, this story has wild places and calmer passages. How does the author set the mood for these different parts of the story? Give examples from the book to support your answer.*

8.   *Think about the meaning of the word desolation. How does that part of the title apply to the story? Consider both the reasons given for the canyon name in the book and other reasons the author may have had for using that word.*

9.   *Lisa is the only girl on the trip. How is her experience the same as or different from everyone else's? How*

would the story have been different if the author had chosen to make the rafters all one gender?

10. How is Aaron's relationship with his father the same as or different from the relationships Lisa and Cassidy have with their dads?

11. What clues did the author give about what happened to Aaron's dad before they found him?

12. Did your opinion of Cassidy change at the end of the story? Why or why not?

13. How is Desolation Canyon similar to another book you've read?

14. At the end of the book, Lisa and Aaron discuss plans for the following summer. What did they decide? What do you think of their decision? Why?

15. What is a major theme of this story? What main ideas do you think the author wants you to take away? Support your ideas with examples from the book.

Best-selling author **Jonathan London** has written more than one hundred picture books for children, many of them about wildlife. He is also the author of the popular Froggy series. He lives with his wife in northern California. www.jonathan-london.net

Sean London was a white-water rafter and a professional dancer while still in high school. He received a BFA from CalArts in Character Animation and has done animation for Disney. *Desolation Canyon* is his first illustrated book, and his first collaboration with his father, Jonathan London. The sequel, *Bella, Bella*, will follow in 2016.